100 Reasons to Celebrate

We invite you to join us in celebrating Mills & Boon's centenary. Gerald Mills and Charles Boon founded Mills & Boon Limited in 1908 and opened offices in London's Covent Garden. Since then, Mills & Boon has become a hallmark for romantic fiction, recognised around the world.

We're proud of our 100 years of publishing excellence, which wouldn't have been achieved without the loyalty and enthusiasm of our authors and readers.

Thank you!

Each month throughout the year there will be something new and exciting to mark the centenary, so watch for your favourite authors, captivating new stories, special limited edition collections...and more!

Dear Reader

It is a very great privilege for me to be personally involved in the celebration of the centenary of Mills & Boon this year. When my first book, HIS INCONVENIENT WIFE, was published in February 2004, I immediately became part of a wonderful stable of talented authors who write exciting, passionate, poignant, inspiring and tender romance novels for readers all over the world.

Our books are translated into twenty-nine different languages and sold in one hundred foreign markets, making Mills & Boon the world's leading publisher of romantic fiction for women. What a stunning achievement it is to have reached the milestone of one hundred years!

I read my first Mills & Boon romance when I was seventeen years old. It was Kay Thorpe's AN APPLE IN EDEN, and it literally changed my life. It was the start of my dream to become a romance author, and while it took me a little while to get there (having been distracted by falling in love and marrying my own Mills & Boon hero first!) I am happy to say I am enjoying every single minute of it.

This book (my twenty-first release), INNOCENT WIFE, BABY OF SHAME, is a novel very dear to my heart. It is a story of reconciliation and forgiveness, and that one thing that has made the world of Mills & Boon go round for the last one hundred years: LOVE.

With warm wishes

Melanie Milburne xx

INNOCENT WIFE, BABY OF SHAME

BY
MELANIE MILBURNE

First published in Great Britain 2007
Harlequin Mills & Boon Limited,
Eton House, 18-24 Paradise Road, Richmond, Surrey TW9 1SR

ISBN: 978 0 263 86406 9

Set in Times Roman 10½ on 12¼ pt
01-0208-51626

Printed and bound in Spain
by Litografia Rosés, S.A., Barcelona

Melanie Milburne says: 'I am married to a surgeon, Steve, and have two gorgeous sons, Paul and Phil. I live in Hobart, Tasmania, where I enjoy an active life as a long-distance runner and a nationally ranked top ten Master's swimmer. I also have a Master's Degree in Education, but my children totally turned me off the idea of teaching! When not running or swimming I write, and when I'm not doing all of the above I'm reading. And if someone could invent a way for me to read during a four-kilometre swim I'd be even happier!'

Recent titles by the same author:

ANDROLETTI'S MISTRESS
WILLINGLY BEDDED, FORCIBLY WEDDED
BOUGHT FOR HER BABY
BEDDED AND WEDDED FOR REVENGE
THE VIRGIN'S PRICE
THE SECRET BABY BARGAIN

The Royal House of Niroli:

SURGEON PRINCE, ORDINARY WIFE *Book 2*

Did you know that Melanie also writes for Medical™ Romance?

HER MAN OF HONOUR
IN HER BOSS'S SPECIAL CARE
A DOCTOR BEYOND COMPARE
A SURGEON WORTH WAITING FOR

This book is dedicated to the memory of my much adored brother-in-law Tom McNamara, who inspired me in so many ways by believing in love and laughter and that most wonderful quality of all—forgiveness. Rest in peace, Tom, and thank you.

CHAPTER ONE

KEIRA did her best to ignore the murmur of speculative voices around her as she travelled on the tram into the city, but it was impossible to ignore the headlines on the front page of the newspaper the man sitting opposite was holding up to read.

Italian multi-millionaire Patrizio Trelini in bitter divorce wrangle with unfaithful wife.

Keira's stomach churned with guilt as the man folded the paper to read the rest of the scandal on page three. She didn't need to get up and look over his shoulder; she knew exactly what was written there. Every day for the last two months her shame had been plastered over every newspaper and every gossip magazine in the country.

The man lowered the paper and looked at her, his eyes narrowing slightly, his lips beginning to thin in contempt.

Keira got off four stops early and, with her shoulders slumping wearily, trudged the rest of the way to where the offices of Trelini Luxury Homes was situated overlooking the sinuous muddy curve of the Yarra River.

She arrived feeling sticky and uncomfortable from the unusually warm early October day, her dark hair in riotous damp curls around her face. She drew in an uneven breath as she made her way through the doors to the reception area where a perfectly groomed and coiffed receptionist sat with a chilly look on her expertly made-up face.

'He won't see you, Mrs Trelini,' Michelle informed Keira brusquely. 'I have been strictly forbidden to put your calls through to him or allow you entry. Now, if you will not leave immediately I am afraid I will have to call security.'

'Please, I—I have to see him,' Keira said, her mouth drying in despair, making it difficult to get the words out. 'It's…it's urgent.'

The receptionist's light blue gaze was disbelieving but after a long tense moment she let out a sigh and reached for the intercom handset. 'Your…er…wife is here to see you,' she said, obviously uncertain how to refer to Keira in the light of what had been going on.

Keira winced when she heard the stream of invective coming from the other end but the receptionist took it in her stride. 'Yes, I know,' she said calmly. 'But she said it's urgent.'

Keira swallowed back her anguish as the receptionist put the handset back down in its cradle a few moments later. 'He will see you when he finishes the call he is currently taking,' she said as she got to her feet. 'I have a tram to catch. Mr Trelini will come and get you when he wants you.'

He doesn't want me. Keira felt the pain of mentally acknowledging the words. She had killed his love for her with one stupid act of reckless defiance.

He was never going to forgive her.

How could he when she couldn't even forgive herself?

Keira sat on the leather sofa in the reception area and looked at the magazines neatly arranged on the coffee table, her heart contracting in despair when she saw that each and every one of them had her guilt and shame splashed over the covers. She reached for the top one, where there was a photo of her leaving Garth Merrick's apartment the morning after she had…

'Hello, Keira.'

The magazine dropped out of her hand as she looked up to see Patrizio standing in front of her. She bent to retrieve it but his foot came over it.

'Leave it.'

She got to her feet, self-consciously tucking a wayward strand of hair back behind her ear. She felt so awkward, so out of place, so unrefined in his presence. She hadn't had time to change after working in the studio and she squirmed as she felt his dark-as-night gaze sweep over her. He was probably thinking she had done it deliberately to annoy him. She could almost feel the censure in his gaze as it burned over every inch of her body.

'I take it the urgent matter you wish to discuss with me has to do with your brother and my nephew,' he said. 'I was just speaking with the headmaster of their school, who informed me of what has been going on.'

Keira rolled her lips together in agitation. 'Yes…I had no idea things had gone that far. I thought they were best friends…in spite of what…what happened…'

His dark brows snapped together. 'How could you think your behaviour would not affect my nephew or indeed your own brother?' he asked incredulously. 'Your salacious affair with Garth Merrick has made me a laughing stock amongst my colleagues and associates, not to mention my family. There is a lot I am prepared to forgive, but not that.'

'I know…' she said, fighting back tears. 'I'm so sorry…'

'Do not waste your breath pretending you are sorry,' he said. 'I am not going to take you back and I am not going to give you the amount of money you are vying for.'

'But I don't want—'

'Forget it, Keira,' he said, cutting her off. 'Right now, you and I need to discuss this situation between the boys like two rational adults, although, having said that, I am very much aware of your limitations in that area.'

'You just can't help yourself, can you?' she asked bitterly. 'You have to have a dig at me every chance you can.'

'This is not the time to discuss my behaviour, Keira, or indeed even yours,' he said with implacable force. 'There is the very real danger of one or both of the boys being expelled during these last critical weeks of school. That is what we need to concentrate on at this point.'

Keira felt ashamed of her outburst; it seemed so petty when he put it like that. 'All right then,' she said, lowering her gaze from the laser strength of his. 'Let's discuss it.'

'Come into my office,' he said. 'I have some coffee brewing.'

She followed him down the wide hall, the fragrant aroma drawing her like a magnet. She had missed breakfast and lunch and, after she had received the call from her mother informing her of Jamie's problems at school, she hadn't had time to grab a snack to tide her over till dinner time. She felt light-headed and faint but somehow she sensed it wasn't just to do with lack of food. Being in Patrizio's presence made her feel out of her depth and desperately vulnerable.

'Do you still have milk and three sugars?' he asked as he took the pot from the stand.

'Do you have artificial sweetener?' she asked.

He turned to look at her, a quizzical expression on his face. 'You are not dieting, are you?'

'Not really…'

She was conscious of his dark eyes assessing her figure and had to fight with herself not to fidget under his scrutiny.

'My secretary has some in the staff room,' he said into the silence. 'I won't be a minute.'

Keira let out her breath in a ragged stream as he left the room. She sat in one of the leather chairs that faced his massive desk, her legs feeling as if the bones had been removed. Her head felt tight with the beginnings of a headache and her stomach was fluttering with a combination of nerves and uncertainty.

Her eyes went to a silver photograph frame on his desk and, leaning forward, she slowly turned it around…

It physically hurt to see the love he'd had for her on their wedding day. His dark eyes had shone with it, his smile tender as he had looked down at her upturned radiant face.

'I keep that as a reminder of what can happen when you marry in haste,' he said as he came back into the room.

Keira turned the frame back around, her chest tightening painfully as she met his black diamond gaze. 'I sort of guessed you wouldn't have it there for sentimental reasons,' she said. 'Will you have a ritual burning of it or will you just toss it out with the garbage once we're finally divorced?'

He handed her the coffee, his fingers briefly touching hers. 'I am glad you brought that topic up,' he said with an enigmatic look.

She put the coffee on the desk, frightened she might spill it. 'I thought we were here to discuss Jamie and Bruno,' she said. 'Not our divorce.'

He sat in his chair behind the desk, his eyes never once leaving hers. 'I am withdrawing my request for a divorce.'

Her eyes widened. 'What?'

He gave her a cool little smile. 'Do not get too excited, Keira. I am not interested in taking you back permanently.'

'I didn't think for a moment you were suggesting—'

'However—' he cut across her as if she hadn't spoken '—I

do think we should temporarily suspend proceedings in an effort to communicate to your brother and my nephew that we are reconciled.'

She gaped at him incredulously. *'Reconciled?'*

'You are unfamiliar with the word?' He leaned back in his chair indolently and explained, 'It means to restore opposing factions to a state of harmony or friendship.'

She threw him a suspicious glance. 'What's all this about, Patrizio?' she asked. 'Why don't you get straight to the point instead of playing these stupid little dictionary games with me?'

'All right,' he said, putting his coffee cup down on the desk as he leaned forward once more. 'As you have no doubt heard, my nephew Bruno has been making life pretty miserable for your brother. I am deeply ashamed of his behaviour, which, I suspect, has come out of his loyalty to me, which of course does not excuse it, but rather explains it.'

Keira remained silent as her hands twisted into tight knots in her lap. It had always amazed her how gracious and forgiving he was towards his own flesh and blood, and yet when it came to her behaviour he could not find it in himself to overlook her one fall from grace.

'I have come to the conclusion that the only way to settle this war between them is for us to get back together,' he continued.

She jerked upright in her seat. 'You mean…for real?'

'No, Keira, I do not mean for real.' His tone yet again mimicked that of an adult speaking to a particularly obtuse and inattentive child. 'We will pretend to be back together until the boys have safely completed their schooling.'

'Pretend?' She frowned at him. 'How do you propose we do that?'

His gaze was unblinking as it held hers. 'You will move back into my house immediately.'

Keira swallowed back her dread. 'You're surely not serious?'

'I am, indeed, very serious, Keira,' he said. 'The boys are not stupid. If we go out on the occasional date in the hope they will think we have settled our differences they will immediately know something is amiss. Living together again as man and wife is the best way to convince them it is for real.'

'Define what you mean by living together as man and wife,' she said, watching him guardedly. 'You're not expecting me to sleep with you, are you?'

'You will have to share my bed due to the regular presence of the household staff,' he said. 'If anyone reported to the press that we were not sharing a bedroom it would blow our cover. However,' he continued, 'I have no intention of sharing my body with you. That is something I no longer have any desire to do.'

His statement hurt far more than he could ever have realised, Keira thought. She felt the pain of his rejection in every nerve and cell in her body. He had desired her so passionately in the past, his body driving into hers with such urgency and potency she had sobbed his name in ecstasy each and every time. Her mind filled with the erotic images of their rocking bodies in every position imaginable. He had taught her so much about sensuality; nothing had been off limits. He had worshipped her as, indeed, she had worshipped him.

Keira became aware of the creeping silence, her face feeling the slow burn of shame spreading over it as she encountered that dark steely gaze.

She hadn't seen him for two months but she had not forgotten how very black his hair was, its loosely controlled style with its slight wave making her ache to run her fingers through it as she had done so many times in the past. His lean jaw was shadowed with the late-in-the-day stubble that marked him as a virile man. His shoulders were broad and his stomach flat and rock-hard from the punishing early morning physical regime he adhered to with the sort of self-discipline she admired but totally lacked herself.

His clothes hung off him with lazy grace, his tie loosened, his shirt undone at his neck giving him an air of casualness that was totally captivating and dangerously attractive.

'You have gone very quiet,' he observed. 'Were you expecting me to ask you to resume an intimate relationship with me?'

Keira moistened the parchment-dryness of her lips. 'No, of course not,' she said. 'I'm just trying to get my head around your suggestion.'

'You do not think it will work?'

She bit at her lip. 'I'm not sure… Won't the boys suspect something when we get back together so suddenly?'

'Not when you recall how quickly we got together in the first place,' he pointed out neatly. 'Remember?'

Keira did and it made her skin tingle from head to foot in reaction. She had met him at a school sports day, her instant attraction to him totally overwhelming. After the final game they had taken the boys out for pizza and, instead of dropping her home, Patrizio had taken her back to his house and made her coffee. Coffee had led to kisses, kisses to caresses and caresses to consummation of their relationship. Keira hadn't had a lover before and had been expecting her first time to be uncomfortable but it was anything but. Her body had responded to his as if it had been fashioned especially for him, the pleasure she had felt in his arms something she would never be able to forget—certainly not now with him sitting so close.

'You haven't answered, Keira,' he said. 'Does that mean you are having trouble recalling our time together or do you save your memory lapses for when you hope it will exonerate you from taking responsibility for your—shall we say—less than honourable actions?'

Keira dragged her gaze back to his, her lips growing tight with anger. She hated herself enough without having him rub her nose in it every chance he could. Couldn't he see how very distressed she was? She had begged for his forgiveness, she had cried and cried and yet he had shunned her totally, refusing to even speak to her other than through his lawyer.

'As you said earlier, we are here to discuss the boys,' she clipped out. 'Could we please stick with that topic?'

He held her gaze for interminable seconds.

'I think the plan will work,' he finally said. 'The boys were once the best of friends. Bruno will hardly continue his appalling behaviour if I tell him I have fallen in love with you again. I suspect that within days of our announcing our intention to resume our marriage they will restore their friendship.'

'But if we resume living together it will delay our divorce,' she said with a worried frown. 'We've been separated for two months. If we live together it will mean we'll have to start from scratch.'

'I realise that, but it cannot be avoided,' he said. 'The boys must be put first over our desire for a divorce.' His eyes probed hers for another lengthy moment. 'Or are you in a particular hurry to process it in order to marry someone else?'

Keira lowered her gaze to her hands in her lap, surprised to see a tiny smear of blood where one of her rough-edged nails had broken the skin. She hadn't felt a thing; the pain she was currently feeling was from much deeper inside. 'No,' she said. 'There's no one else.'

'Fine,' he said. 'That means we can get going on this without delay.'

Keira sat in silence, still twisting her hands and worrying her bottom lip with her teeth.

'Do not worry about your parents,' he said after a little pause.

She looked up at him and frowned. 'You've already discussed this with them?'

'No,' he said. 'But I am well aware of your strained relationship with them.'

Keira couldn't help the rush of feeling that surged through her at his softened tone. He had always understood her difficulties relating to her strait-laced and conservative parents, and had often protected her from their criticism in the past. That had been one of the things she had missed most about him. He had been her defender, her rock and fortress. She had felt so alone without him in her life—so achingly and desperately alone.

'Of course, while we are involved in this charade, it goes without saying that any involvement with other parties must immediately cease,' he said.

Keira shifted her gaze again. 'I'm not involved with anyone.'

'Good,' he said. 'I am between relationships as well so the timing is perfect.'

Keira had seen a photograph in the press of his new lover. Gisela Hunter was the total opposite of her—a tall platinum blonde-haired beauty, with rail-thin arms and legs and the sort of smile the cost of which must have put a Ferrari in some top-notch orthodontist's garage.

She fought down her jealousy and reminded herself that she had no one but herself to blame. She had jumped to conclusions and, in her normal impulsive way, had acted on a suspicion that in the end had proved to be incorrect.

'I understand that you are currently working part-time at a café,' he said.

She brought her eyes back to his. 'Yes. It helps to pay my rent and for my painting materials.'

'You will give the café proprietor your notice immediately,' he said. 'I will pay you a wage for the duration of our mock reconciliation.'

'You don't have to do that…'

'No, but I will do it all the same. I cannot have people wondering why you are slaving over a coffee machine when your husband is a multi-millionaire.'

She looked down at her hands again, knowing it would be pointless refusing. He wouldn't take no for an answer and, besides, she needed money; her rent was already two weeks in arrears. 'All right…' she said, 'if you insist.'

She heard the creak of leather as he leaned forward in his chair and she looked up to meet his eyes, her stomach giving a little shuffling movement at the dark intensity she could see reflected there.

'This is not about us, Keira,' he said. 'It is about two young boys on the threshold of adulthood who are jeopardising their futures with unnecessary bitterness.'

Her tongue moved over the dryness of her lips again. 'I understand…'

'Good,' he said. 'Then you will also understand the urgency of making an announcement to the press.' He picked up his mobile from his desk and, scrolling through, pressed the name that came up on the dial.

She listened as he informed the journalist at the other end that, as of tonight, Keira and Patrizio Trelini had cancelled their acrimonious divorce proceedings and were resuming their relationship.

Indefinitely…

CHAPTER TWO

PATRIZIO put the phone back down and faced her. 'How soon can you move back into my place?'

Her stomach tilted again. 'Um…'

'Would it help if I sent Marietta over to pack your things?'

She nodded, not trusting her voice to come out without a break in it. He wasn't just doing this for his nephew; he was doing it for Jamie as well. Somehow she found that particularly touching.

'I will need to give Marietta the keys to your flat,' he said, passing her a piece of paper and a pen. 'Jot down what you think you will need for the next six weeks and she and Salvatore will sort it out this evening.'

Keira gripped the pen and tried to think about what she would need in order to play the role of reconciled wife but it was difficult to concentrate with him sitting so close. The air circulating between them held a faint trace of his lemon-scented aftershave, which made her feel as if he were touching her in a vicarious way. She was breathing him in, breath by ragged breath, and it disturbed her deeply.

'I think we should have dinner together tonight,' he said once she'd passed him the list and her keys. 'It will give credence to our announcement to the press.'

Keira looked down at her paint-splattered clothes. 'I need to get changed…'

'There are still some of your clothes at my house.'

Her eyes came up to meet his. 'You mean you haven't thrown them all out?'

He gave her one of his unreadable looks. 'Marietta insisted they were to stay in the wardrobe until the divorce was finalised. I think she has always hoped you would come back.'

She looked down at her hands again. 'Did you tell her you wouldn't *have* me back?' she asked.

It seemed a long time before he answered. Keira could hear the clock on the wall behind her counting out the seconds; they seemed to be out of time with her thumping heart.

'I told her what we had was well and truly over,' he said. 'I did not discuss the details with her or with anyone, although she could hardly have avoided hearing about it in the press. The journalists are still having a field day with it, no doubt because of your father's bid for the Senate.'

Keira knew she should be feeling grateful that he hadn't revealed the sordid details of her betrayal with all and sundry. He had had every right to do so—what she had done had been unforgivable. She could only assume that he had remained silent out of a sense of male pride. He would deem it below him to reveal the particulars of his private life, although she couldn't help wondering why he had all those magazines in the waiting room. Perhaps, like the wedding photo on his desk, he wanted to remind himself of how he had been let down by someone he had once trusted and loved.

He passed the phone to her. 'I think you should call your brother at school,' he said. 'It would be better for him to hear it from you rather than read it in the papers tomorrow.'

Keira stared at the phone in her hands. Could she lie convincingly to her younger brother? Although eight years separated them, she and Jamie had always been exceptionally close.

She pressed the numbers and waited for him to pick up his mobile.

'Hello?'

'Jamie, it's me, Keira.'

'Hi, Keira, how are you doing? How are the paintings going for the exhibition?'

'Not so bad,' she said, trying to lift her tone. 'How are you?'

There was a tiny pause.

'OK, I guess…'

'Jamie,' she began, 'I have something to tell you.'

'You're not going to marry Garth Merrick, are you?' he asked, the edge of panic unmistakable in his tone.

Keira had to turn away from the quirked-brow look Patrizio sent her as her brother's voice carried across the room. 'No, of course not. We're just…friends.'

'What is it, then?'

She took a calming breath. 'Patrizio and I have decided to get back together,' she said, mentally crossing her fingers that he would buy it.

'The divorce is off?'

'Yes,' she said. 'The divorce is off.'

'Wow, Keira, that's great!' he said excitedly. 'What brought this about?'

'I guess we both realised we were making a big mistake,' she said, adlibbing as she went along. 'We both still love each other, so a divorce is pointless.'

'I'm so glad, Keira,' he said. 'You haven't been happy since…well, since it all fell apart. What do Mum and Dad think? Have you told them yet?'

'Not yet, but I'll call them next.'

There was another little silence.

'Does Bruno Di Venuto know?' Jamie asked.

Keira met Patrizio's eyes across the desk. 'No,' she said. 'But Patrizio is about to ring him.'

'I saw him in the common room a few minutes ago,' Jamie said. 'He was his usual obnoxious self.'

'Has it been very difficult for you, Jamie?' she asked. 'You haven't mentioned a thing in any of the calls we've had lately.'

'I can handle him, Keira,' Jamie said. 'He's got a chip on his shoulder about you and his uncle divorcing. He thinks it's all your fault but I told him you only did what you did because you thought Patrizio was having an affair. You weren't to know you were being set up. Anyone could have made the same mistake.'

Keira inwardly cringed. 'I'm sorry you've had to suffer because of me,' she said. 'I wish I could have avoided dragging you into my problems.'

'Don't be daft,' he responded. 'You always stuck up for me when Mum and Dad got angry about some stupid little issue. But I must say I'm glad to hear your news. I really want to do well in the finals and the way Bruno has been carrying on was making life pretty difficult. He's got some influential mates. My grades have been falling but I should be able to pick them up if he lays off a bit.'

Keira met Patrizio's dark unblinking gaze across the desk. 'Patrizio assures me Bruno will,' she said. 'Take care of yourself, Jamie. I love you.'

'Don't go all soppy on me now,' he said gruffly. 'I am really pleased you and Patrizio are having another go at it. I like him, Keira. I always did. He's one really cool dude.'

Keira handed the phone back to Patrizio a short time later. 'Apparently, in spite of your nephew's behaviour, my brother still thinks you're one really cool dude.'

He gave her an indifferent look. 'So I heard.'

She listened while he made a call to his nephew and, even though it was issued in staccato Italian, she more or less got the drift. Patrizio's brows snapped together as he ranted and railed, the gestures of his hand indicating that he was extremely angry.

He put the phone down on the desk a few minutes later with a brooding frown. 'That boy needs a firm hand. I should have seen this coming. I could have stopped it getting to this.'

'It's all right, Patrizio,' she said. 'Jamie is coping with things.'

He got to his feet and stood with his back to her, looking out over the city below. 'I cannot be the father figure Bruno needs,' he said, clenching and unclenching his fists by his sides. 'I have tried to take Stefano's place but it is not good enough. No one can replace his father. Bruno is angry and resentful and is no doubt looking for a target.'

'You have done your best,' she said softly. 'It's been hard for everyone, Gina especially.'

He turned around to look down at her. 'We should get going,' he said after a stiff little silence. He scooped up his keys from the desk and added, 'The sooner we get this over with the better.'

Keira followed him out of the office with a sinking feeling in her stomach. Spending the evening with him was going to be bad enough, but sharing his house as his wife again was going to take all the courage she possessed and more.

Patrizio's house was a modern mansion set in a private garden in the exclusive suburb of South Yarra. Large windows made the most of the view over the city on one side and the lap pool and beautifully manicured formal garden on the other.

Italian marble lined the impressive foyer, leading to a

sweeping staircase which led to the upper floor where each of the beautifully decorated bedrooms had an *en suite* bathroom attached. Soft-as-air taupe carpet covered the living and entertainment areas, the luxurious leather sofas just begging to be sat upon.

Keira forced her gaze away from them, not wanting to recall the many times she had felt and tasted his passion while lying entangled with him there.

'I will leave you to get changed,' Patrizio said as he put his briefcase down. 'I have a couple of emails to send. Make yourself at home.'

This used to be my home, Keira thought sadly as she took the stairs to the upper floor. Every room contained a memory of her time with Patrizio. It seemed strange to be here again, walking up the stairs as if she had never left.

She paused outside the master bedroom, taking a little shaky breath as her hand pushed open the door.

She forced her eyes away from the huge bed and went straight to the large walk-in wardrobe where on one side Patrizio's things were hanging in neat ordered rows.

Her gaze swung to the other side and a little wave of nostalgia passed over her as her hands went to the things she had left behind. The housekeeper, Marietta, had obviously tidied everything up. Admittedly Keira had left in a hurry after that final horrendous scene, but then she had never been all that good at keeping things organised.

Her hand reached for one of the dresses Patrizio had bought her when they had gone to Paris for a week during the first few months of their marriage. She pressed her face against it, her eyes closing as she felt the soft brush of chiffon against her cheek, the faint hint of his aftershave clinging to the fabric making her feel an unbearable aching emptiness.

She heard a sound behind her and came face to face with

Marietta, who was carrying a bundle of Patrizio's neatly ironed casual clothes.

'Signora Trelini,' she said with a smile. 'It is good to see you again. I am so glad you are returning to Signor Trelini. He has not been happy since you left.'

'Hello, Marietta,' Keira said shyly, still clutching the dress to her chest. 'I haven't been happy since I left either.'

The housekeeper beamed. 'I knew it would all work out in the end,' she said. 'You and Signor Trelini are…how you say…soul mates, *sì*?'

'*Sì*,' Keira agreed, hoping she sounded convincing.

Marietta put the clothes she was carrying on the shelves before turning back to her. 'I will leave you to get dressed,' she said. 'Your husband told me you are going out to dinner to celebrate your reconciliation.'

'Er…yes…we are,' Keira said.

'I have left towels in the *en suite* for you,' Marietta informed her. 'I thought you might like to freshen up.'

'Thank you, Marietta,' Keira said, grimacing as she looked down at her jeans. 'A shower would be lovely.'

The stinging spray did much to wash away the stickiness of the day, the creamy shampoo and conditioner she used on her hair leaving it bouncing with springy curls.

She looked at her reflection and bit her lip. There were shadows beneath her violet-blue eyes and her face looked even paler than it usually was. She leaned closer and frowned when she saw the dusting of freckles on the bridge of her nose. Her small supply of make-up was at her poky little flat in St Kilda; all she had was a tub of lip-gloss in her purse.

She smoothed down the black dress and, slipping her feet into the high-heeled sandals she'd chosen, she went back downstairs.

Patrizio was waiting for her in the large open-plan lounge,

a small measure of spirits in his hand. 'Would you care for a drink before we leave?' he asked.

Keira wondered what he would say if she told him she no longer touched alcohol. She hadn't dared after what had happened with Garth. 'No, thank you,' she said. 'I had some water upstairs.'

His eyes ran over her. 'You look very beautiful, *cara*,' he said.

She shifted nervously. 'Thank you…'

He closed the distance between them and lifted her chin, his eyes burning into hers. 'Marietta and Salvatore have not yet left,' he said in a low deep undertone. 'We are in love again, no?'

'No…I mean yes…' Keira answered, her heart beginning to thump as his thumb moved over her bottom lip, back and forth as if rediscovering the cushioned contours.

He pressed his mouth to hers for a nanosecond before lifting his head, his tongue sweeping over his lips where she could see a faint imprint of her lip-gloss shining.

'Mmm,' he said, running his tongue over his lips. 'You taste of strawberries, or is it cherries?'

Keira felt her belly tremble with desire as he bent his head once more. Her lashes came down over her eyes as his mouth covered hers, the barely there touch of his lips sending her senses into a frenzy. She felt the slight rasp of his tongue as it pushed against the seam of her mouth, her stomach giving a swift hard kick of excitement as the pressure subtly increased. Her lips parted to accommodate him, the smooth gliding entry of his tongue making every hair on her head stand to attention as it flicked against hers.

That first erotic thrust sent all thought of control out of her head. Her hands clung to him unashamedly, her fingers curling into the front of his shirt, her mouth locked on his, her tongue dancing with his in a sexy tango that mimicked the most intimate union of all.

She could feel the heavy pulse of desire beating deep and low in her body, every nerve tightening in tingling awareness as his mouth worked its magic on hers. She felt the hard ridge of his erection swelling against her belly, the heady reminder of all they had shared in the past.

Keira vaguely registered the sound of the front door closing and her eyes sprang open when Patrizio ended the kiss with an abruptness she found totally disorienting.

'Marietta and Salvatore have gone,' he said, stepping back from her. 'I was expecting one or both of them to come in and say good evening. The kiss was for their benefit, not mine.'

Keira ran her tongue over her still tingling lips. 'I see…'

He sent her one of his inscrutable looks. 'We will have to perform from time to time,' he said. 'I would not want you to misinterpret anything in such physical exchanges.'

She swallowed back her pain. 'I understand…'

'Good,' he said, his eyes dipping to her mouth briefly before returning to hers. 'As long as we both know how things stand.'

'I understand you hate me,' Keira said. 'You've made it pretty clear.'

A hard glitter came into his eyes as they clashed with hers. 'Do I not have the right to hate you, Keira?' he asked. 'You destroyed our marriage by sleeping with another man.'

Keira closed her eyes tight, unable to look at the fury in his black-brown gaze.

His hands gripped her upper arms. 'Look at me, damn you!'

Her eyes sprang open, tears burning as she encountered the bitterness reflected in his gaze. 'I'm s-sorry…' she whispered brokenly. 'I'm so sorry…'

He dropped his hands and let out a muttered curse. 'I suppose you are going to spin me that worn-out excuse that you had too much to drink and did not know what you were doing,' he said.

'I wasn't drinking…' she said, unable to meet the burning accusation in his eyes. 'Or at least no more than half a glass…but it's true that I don't really remember much about that night…apart from the argument we had and…and going to Garth's place…'

'Where you opened your legs for him like the filthy little slut you are,' he ground out savagely, his black brows meeting over his eyes.

Keira felt her shame scorch her from head to foot. If she hadn't woken up naked in Garth's bed the next morning, she would never have believed herself capable of such reckless behaviour. But, even worse, she hadn't just betrayed her husband, but the one friend who had stood by her for most of her childhood.

'Did he make you sob with ecstasy, Keira?' he asked. 'Did he make you beg for release the way you begged for it with me? *Did he?*'

She put her hands over her ears. 'Don't. Please. I can't bear it!'

He pulled her hands down, his fingers biting into her wrists. 'Did you put him in your mouth like you did to me? Did you—'

Keira felt herself begin to sway on her feet, her face draining of colour as the room began to spin uncontrollably. She tried to focus on his embittered words but they faded away as if he were speaking to her through a very long and fog-filled tunnel. She tried to get her voice to work but her throat felt as if someone had lodged something hard halfway down. She felt her body begin to slump against his, her extremities tingling as if every drop of her blood had completely drained out of her.

'Keira?'

She opened her eyes at the gruff urgency of his tone but had to close them again as the black abyss inexorably beckoned…

CHAPTER THREE

KEIRA woke to find herself lying in Patrizio's bed, the covers lightly over her, the bedside lamp casting an incandescent glow over the room.

'How are you feeling?' he asked from the chair beside the bed.

She turned her head on the pillow and met his dark concerned gaze. 'I…I'm fine…I think…'

'You fainted,' he said somewhat unnecessarily.

'Yes…'

'Has that happened before?' he asked.

'A couple of times…' she answered, putting a hand up to brush her hair out of her face. 'I had the flu a few weeks ago…I haven't fully recovered.'

'When did you last eat?'

'I don't remember…last night, I think.'

He swore and got to his feet. 'How long has this being going on?' he asked.

'I don't see why you should be concerned,' she said with a glittering look. 'You hate me, remember? Why should you care whether I eat or not?'

'I am concerned, as anyone would be, when the person one is speaking with suddenly drops in a dead faint before them,' he responded. 'It is disconcerting, to say the least.'

'Then maybe you shouldn't speak to them so aggressively,' she countered.

He frowned down at her. 'I suppose this is how you handle difficult conversations now, is it?' he asked. 'When things get a bit hot to handle, you block it out by bringing on a fainting episode.'

Keira jerked upright in the bed, her eyes flashing at him in fury. 'I did not bring on anything! I told you, I've been sick recently. I haven't felt well for a month, if you must know.'

There was a taut little silence.

'Are you pregnant?' he asked.

She stared at him in shock. 'What sort of question is that?' she asked. 'Of course I'm not pregnant.'

'I would have thought it was a reasonable one to ask,' he said. 'You are a young sexually active woman.'

'I am not sexually active. I haven't had sex since…' she paused as she bit her lip '…since that night…'

His expression communicated his disbelief. 'You positively ooze sex, Keira. As soon as you walked into my office, I could feel it coming off you like an invisible force.'

She moistened her mouth as his dark gaze slid over her in indolent appraisal. Her breasts tightened and her stomach hollowed and clenched simultaneously.

'You are a very sensual woman, Keira,' he continued. 'There are few men who could resist what you have to offer.'

'I'm not offering anything.'

His lip curled. 'I bet if I got into that bed beside you I could have you underneath me screaming out in ecstasy within minutes. You just cannot help yourself. You are built for pleasure, *cara*. I am getting hard just thinking about it.'

Keira couldn't stop her eyes going to his pelvis. A tremor of desire rumbled through her belly and her heart began to step up its pace.

He came to sit on the edge of her bed, right next to her thighs, one of his hands capturing hers and laying it against his throbbing heat. 'Can you feel what you do to me, Keira?'

She could and it terrified her. Her fingers itched to explore and the barrier of his clothes became a torment. She wanted to feel that satin-covered steel against her fingertips. She wanted to taste that sexy combination of salt and musk on his skin, to feel his explosive release in every intimate place.

'B-but you hate me,' she said, trying to pull her hand away without success.

'Yes, but it does not interfere with my desire for you; in fact, I believe it might even enhance it.'

'That's barbaric,' she said, giving her hand another vicious tug. 'Besides, I thought you said you didn't intend to share your body with me. You told me you no longer felt any attraction towards me.'

He brought her hand up to his mouth, his tongue tasting each of her fingertips in turn, his smouldering dark gaze locked with hers. 'Let us say I am considering the fors and againsts,' he said.

'What you need to be considering is my consent,' she put in archly.

His mouth tilted in a mocking smile. 'You have already given me your consent,' he said. 'We are still legally married, remember?'

'We're officially separated.'

'Not any more.'

'This isn't a real reconciliation,' she said, panic beating like a drum in her chest. 'You told me it wasn't.'

'In the eyes of the law, it is. We have resumed cohabiting as man and wife.'

'I don't want to be your wife, either for real or pretend,' she said with stiff force. 'I don't want to live with a man who hates me with every breath he takes. I can think of nothing worse.'

'I do not know why you are so upset. You were the one to destroy our marriage.'

'I didn't do it alone!' she cried.

'No, indeed you did not,' he said coolly, although his dark gaze burned with anger. 'You did it with Garth Merrick.'

'I didn't mean that,' she said, blowing out a breath of frustration. 'I meant I wouldn't have even gone to Garth in the first place if I hadn't thought you were having an affair.'

'Oh, yes,' he said with another mocking curl of his lip. 'My alleged affair.'

Keira felt perilously close to tears. She hated being reminded of her stupidity back then. She had been insanely jealous but too proud to admit to it, and instead had allowed a vindictive woman to systematically poison her against the man she loved with all her heart.

At the time their barely twelve-month-old marriage had been going through a particularly rocky patch, which with hindsight she realised was entirely normal. Two strong-willed people living together were sure to send sparks flying at times, especially when he had been busy with a big housing deal interstate, and she was snowed under with her studies. And with her propensity to fly off the handle so easily, not to mention her deep-seated insecurity stemming from her childhood, it had been a ripe field for the seeds of suspicion to be sown.

Rita Favore had deliberately fed her suspicions, leaving suggestive messages on the land line answering service and even producing photographs which had later been proven to be digitally adjusted to make them appear more intimate than they really were. Keira had been so devastated, seeing her husband in such a compromising embrace, she hadn't stopped to think of an alternative explanation.

Patrizio had been in Sydney on business when she'd called him and accused him of being unfaithful. He had denied it vehemently but she hadn't believed him. She had hung up on him and taken the phone off the hook and switched her mobile off for several hours.

When he'd returned that evening she had already packed her things and was waiting for him in the lounge.

'You are surely not serious about this, *cara*?' he asked as soon as she told him she was leaving. 'I hardly know the woman. She works for me—yes, but only as a part-time assistant.'

Keira sent him a livid blue glare. 'Assisting you part-time with what?' She shoved the photos at him. 'With enhancing your sex life?'

His frown increased as he leafed through each of the incriminating photographs. He tossed them to the nearest surface and faced her, his expression incredulous. 'Keira, this is ridiculous. This is obviously some sort of attempt to discredit me, but I can assure you I have never slept with that woman.'

'She left several messages for you. Why don't you listen to them?'

He brushed past her to pick up the phone and, punching in the message retrieval code, frowned as he listened.

Keira put her hands on her hips. 'Well?' she said. 'Are you still going to blatantly deny it?'

He put the phone down with unnecessary force, his eyes almost black with anger. 'How can you think me capable of betraying you with such a woman?' he asked. 'She is so very obviously making trouble. I have never touched her. I would not dream of doing so.'

'I don't believe you.'

His eyes went to her suitcases, his expression wry. 'Obviously not.'

'I want a divorce,' she said, putting up her chin in defiance. 'I don't want to be married to you any more.'

His dark eyes took on a steely glint. 'Is that so?'

'Yes. I should never have married you in the first place.'

'Why is that, I wonder?' he asked, stepping closer.

Keira tried to step backwards but came up against the door, the sensation of being cornered triggering a primal response to escape. 'Because I'm in love with someone else,' she said.

Her words dropped like a bomb into the silence, splintering it into a million fragments of fury as Patrizio's eyes narrowed into black slits.

'What did you say?' he asked in a low deep growl.

Her chin went even higher. 'You heard me. I'm in love with someone else.'

'Who is it?' he asked. 'Or am I allowed to guess?'

She held his laser-like gaze with glittering rebellion. 'I don't have to tell you anything if I don't want to.'

His mouth tightened into a thin white line. 'How long have you been in love with him?'

Keira had dug herself in so deeply she decided she might as well go for broke. 'I have loved him all my life,' she said. 'I'm going to him now.'

Something seemed to snap in him at her words. He pulled her towards him, his mouth slamming down on hers, his arms like steel bands around her. The sheer animal intensity of it caught her off guard. Instead of pushing him away, she got swept away in the rough urgency of it. She kissed him back with blazing passionate heat, her teeth biting at him. She wanted him, needed him. He spun her around, her hands flat against the door, her skirt hitched up around her waist, the tiny barrier of her lacy knickers shoved to one side as he drove into her slick moistness with fast-paced deep thrusts that had her whimpering in pleasure within seconds.

She was still trying to get her breathing back in order when he withdrew from her. She slowly turned around, hot colour coursing through her at her own wanton weakness.

'That should give you something to remember me by,' he said in a flinty tone as he re-zipped his trousers.

And, with one last raking look, he left her standing there with the scent of her shame lingering in the air.

CHAPTER FOUR

KEIRA was jerked back to the present when Patrizio got up from the bed. She watched as he paced the room, his hand going through the black silk of his hair, leaving it ruffled and disordered and devastatingly sexy.

'My alleged affair,' he repeated, his tone full of derision. 'I thought you of all people had more sense than to be fooled by someone using computer Photoshop techniques that even a child could use.'

Keira felt herself cringing in shame. She had been so stupid, so blind with jealousy, she hadn't taken the time to think things through rationally. 'I'm sorry…' she said, biting her lip until she could taste blood. 'I wouldn't have fallen for it if it hadn't been for the messages as well. She rang the whole time you were away. I couldn't help thinking the worst…'

He turned around to glare at her. 'How could you do it to us, Keira?' he asked. 'I loved you so much. I would have given my life for you.'

Tears sprang from her eyes, her chest feeling far too tight to breathe. The knife of guilt twisting even further.

'You were away so much,' she said in a desperate attempt to justify her unjustifiable actions. 'I couldn't help being suspicious.'

'You were suspicious because you were looking for a way out,' he said. 'You were in love with Merrick all the time.'

'No!' She got to her feet unsteadily. 'I was lying when I said that to you. I didn't love him…or at least not in that way.'

'But you still slept with him.'

She had to look away. 'Yes…'

'We could have sorted it out,' he said, his voice hoarse with held-back emotion. 'Within twenty-four hours we could have sorted it out.'

She gulped back a sob and nodded. 'I know…'

She heard him release a ragged sigh. 'I cannot forgive you for what you did, Keira,' he said. 'I have tried to, but I just cannot do it.'

'I understand…' Keira bowed her head in shame. Pain racked her being; every joint seemed to ache with it.

'You were intent on paying me back for an affair I did not have,' he went on. 'You did not stop to think of the consequences, you just went right ahead and ripped my heart out of my chest.'

'I only did it the once,' she said in her defence. 'And, if it's any comfort to you, I don't even remember a lot of that night.'

He gave her a scathing look. 'What sort of twisted mind do you have that you think that would somehow make it less offensive?' he asked. 'For God's sake, Keira, you gave your body to another man. Do you really expect me to forgive and forget? I *cannot* do it. Every time I look at you I think of that creep's hands on you and his body inside yours.'

'He's not a creep…' she said with a tiny spark of defiance in her gaze.

The ensuing silence stretched and stretched to snapping point, every single beat of it like a hammer blow to her heart as his dark eyes bored like twin drills into the tender flesh of her soul.

She closed her eyes. This was too much. She couldn't cope with this avalanche of feeling.

'I *loved* you, Keira,' he said, the slight break in his voice making guilt assail her all over again. 'You killed that love.'

'I know…I don't blame you…what I did was unforgivable. I can't even forgive myself…'

Patrizio moved to the other side of the room and stared sightlessly out of the window. He had prepared himself for her defiance, not her despair. She looked pale and vulnerable, as if her world had collapsed around her. It reawakened every protective instinct he had felt for her from the first moment he had met her. Her beguiling mix of wild child and sensual woman had been a devastatingly attractive package. He had broken all his rules and married her within weeks of meeting her. But it didn't matter what desire still leapt between them now—the reminder of how she had given herself to someone else would stay with him for ever.

He had never been able to remove the vision of her lying naked in Garth Merrick's bed. The morning after their heated argument, he had felt a little ashamed of how he had reacted to her request for a divorce, realising with hindsight that it was probably just a knee-jerk response. When he'd cooled down at bit he conceded she had been justifiably upset. The photos were very well done, and given the context of Keira's deep-seated insecurity, which he knew stemmed from her difficult relationship with her father, it would be all too easy for her to think she had been betrayed. He wanted to find her and apologise for not taking her concerns more seriously, but instead of finding her taking shelter with her friend, she had done the very last thing he had expected her to do.

It still made nausea rise like a thick hot tide in his stomach when he thought of the gloating pride on Merrick's face as he'd greeted him at the door of his flat…

'Where is my wife?' Patrizio ground out.

'She's in bed,' Garth said with a combative look. 'She doesn't want to see you, Trelini.'

'But I want to see her,' Patrizio said, pushing the door back against the wall with a vicious slap of wood on plaster.

He had found the bedroom without any trouble as it was the only one in the flat. And inside it he found his wife lying totally naked on the bed, her body sprawled like a whore's, her eyes closed in blissful unawareness of his presence.

'Don't wake her,' Garth said from behind him, his voice low. 'She had a migraine. She was sick for hours.'

Patrizio clenched and unclenched his fists. He wanted to shake her awake, to drag her by the hair out of her lover's bed, but he knew it would be pointless. Hatred burned like a forest fire in his belly and he swore he would never set eyes on her again.

And he hadn't.

Until today.

Patrizio slowly turned around to find her sitting with her head bowed, the bitten nails of one hand picking at the skin near her cuticles on the other. She looked pale and fragile, like a bird that had had its wings clipped and was struggling to fly again.

She lifted her head as if she had sensed his gaze on her and her pale cheeks slowly filled with delicate colour. He saw the up and down movement of her throat and the way the tip of her tongue came out to brush a film of moisture over her lips.

He had to harden his resolve all over again. He had known it would be hard, but not this hard. He hadn't expected it to hurt so much to see her. It physically hurt to look at her. Pain knifed through him, like a thousand scalpels reopening old wounds that had taken every single day of the two months of their separation to start to heal over.

'Patrizio…' Her voice was so soft he almost didn't hear it, but he saw her mouth moving and suddenly realised she was speaking. 'I—I want to thank you for doing this to help the boys…I know it's not what either of us wants. I just want you to know I'll try and do my best to make sure it works.'

'Thank you,' he said, surprised that his voice sounded so even when he'd had to drag it past a golf ball–sized lump in his throat. 'It was all I could think of to resolve the situation.'

'It's only for six weeks…'

'Yes.'

He looked away, unable to hold her wounded violet-blue gaze any longer. 'If you are not feeling well enough to eat out this evening we can postpone it until tomorrow evening,' he said. 'One day will not make much difference either way.'

'I'll be fine,' she said. 'I'm feeling much better now. Besides, I need to eat something.'

He moved to the other side of the room and, taking a small envelope off the coffee table, came back across and handed it to her.

Keira looked at it warily. 'What is it?'

His eyes were steady on hers. 'Your wedding and engagement rings,' he said.

She took the envelope with fingers that felt numb and useless. 'You kept them?'

He gave an indolent shrug. 'I hadn't got around to selling them after you sent them back to me. I was waiting until the divorce was finalised.'

She bit her lip and slowly took them out of the envelope, the crackle of the stiff paper sounding like someone stepping on bubble wrap. The rings lay in her palm, shining up at her with glittering eyes of accusation.

'You had better put them on and keep them on while we are acting out this charade,' he said into the silence. 'Once it is over, you can keep them or send them back to me as you did the last time. I do not care either way.'

He turned to pick up his keys from the coffee table, the noise of them jangling against each other more like the sound of clanging bells in the thick silence.

Keira got to her feet, her legs still feeling shaky, but somehow she managed to follow him from the room and out to the car.

He didn't talk on the way to the restaurant he had booked on Toorak Road. She glanced at him once or twice, her heart contracting as she saw his clenched jaw and tight mouth and the dark shadows beneath his eyes.

She let out a tiny sigh and wished she could turn back the clock. How different things might have been if that night had never happened. But it had and she had no way of undoing the damage. Even Garth had drifted away from her; their lifelong friendship had never quite recovered from that stolen night of passion.

Patrizio parked the car and came around to open her door, the cooler night air lifting the bare skin of her arms into tiny goose-bumps. 'Are you cold?' he asked, sliding his hand down the length of her arm to capture one of her hands in his.

Keira felt the latent strength in his fingers, her blood thrumming in her veins at the thought of feeling his touch all over her body once more. Her most secret place moistened and pulsed with longing to feel his hard presence plunging inside her again.

'N-no…' she said, shivering as his thumb moved back and forth over the leaping pulse under the translucent skin of her wrist.

He held her gaze for a moment, his expression hard to read. She felt his thumb come to a standstill, as if he were measuring the thud, thud, thud of her blood racing beneath her skin.

'You are nervous, *cara*?' he asked.

Keira wished he wouldn't keep using those wonderful Italian terms of endearment he had used so often in the past. It didn't seem right now when he hated her so much. 'A bit,' she said. 'I'm not sure I can do this now it comes to the crunch.'

'We have eaten together many times in the past, Keira,' he reminded her. 'Let us pretend the last two months did not happen. It will be much better that way.'

He led her into the restaurant, where they were greeted by the *maître d'*. 'Mr Trelini and Mrs Trelini!' His eyes lit up. 'What is this? I cannot believe my very own eyes. You are having dinner together?'

'Yes,' Patrizio said. 'We are celebrating our reconciliation.'

'Congratulations!' the *maître d'* gushed. 'That is wonderful, eh? No nasty divorce and no greedy lawyers.'

'Right,' Patrizio said with a smile and expression that spoke volumes.

Keira felt herself mentally recoiling at how obstructive she had been over the divorce. The female lawyer representing her had encouraged her to push for a fifty-fifty settlement and, although she hated doing so, she had agreed. It had been a desperate measure on her part as she knew Patrizio would fight it every inch of the way, but at least their divorce wouldn't be finalised until they reached some sort of agreement. She'd rationalised that it would give her a few extra weeks to try and get him to reconsider his refusal to forgive her. It wasn't as if she wanted Patrizio's money; she had wanted his love and forgiveness much more than any amount of wealth.

They were shown to their table and left with the wine list. 'Do you want red or white wine?' Patrizio asked as he began to peruse the list.

'I'd better stick to mineral water,' she said, fidgeting with her purse. 'I don't want to trigger a headache.'

He lowered the list to look at her, a shadow of concern in his dark gaze. 'Have you had more migraines than usual lately?'

She found it hard to keep her emotions in check with his coal-black eyes on hers. 'Yes...' she said, dropping her gaze from his. 'It's stress related mostly. I've got some pills to take now...they help a lot...'

Just then a man approached with a camera, a woman at his side with a notebook and pen.

'Mr Trelini—' the young woman spoke first '—we've heard a rumour today that you and Mrs Trelini are resuming your marriage.'

'Yes, that is true,' Patrizio said with an urbane smile. 'We are indeed resuming our marriage and are both very happy to be together again.'

'So does this mean you've forgiven your wife for her affair with Garth Merrick?' she asked with a meaningful glance in Keira's direction.

Keira felt her face fill with colour as if her shame had overflowed from deep inside to find a more public place to showcase itself.

'But of course,' Patrizio said. 'We are all entitled to one mistake, no? Many men have strayed in the past and their wives have been expected to not only forgive but to turn a blind eye. What is sauce for the goose and all that, right?'

'Er...right,' the journalist said, madly scribbling.

The man with the camera came closer and asked them to pose. Keira stretched her mouth into a semblance of a smile, the tiny fine hairs on the back of her neck lifting one by one as Patrizio's hand cupped her nape.

'Thank you both,' the journalist said. 'Enjoy your evening.'

'We will,' Patrizio said with another charming smile.

Keira blew out a ragged little sigh once they had left. 'I'm not very good at this…'

'You did fine,' he said. 'Now, what are you going to eat?'

Keira had never felt less like eating in her life. She stared at the menu for endless minutes, chewing at her bottom lip, wondering if he had any idea of how much this was affecting her.

He reached across the table and lifted her chin with his hand, the pad of his thumb moving over her savaged bottom lip. 'You will draw blood if you keep doing that, *cara*,' he said.

Tears shone in her eyes as she held his dark fathomless gaze. 'I c-can't help it…' She choked back a tiny sob.

She heard him draw in a sharp breath, his fingers moving to cup her cheek in a touch so gentle and tender that the tears she was desperately trying to hold back began to spill from her eyes.

'Please do not cry, Keira,' he said. 'Does my presence upset you this much?'

She nodded as another little broken sob escaped. 'Sorry…I'll be fine in a minute…'

'You need feeding,' he said, signalling for the waiter.

Keira mopped at her eyes as she heard Patrizio order her favourite dish for her, the fragile hold she had on her emotions threatening to slip away again. He might not love her but he hadn't forgotten what she liked and disliked. Somehow she found that comforting.

'How are your studies going?' he asked once the waiter had left. 'You must be close to finishing.'

'Yes…' she said, conscious of the steadiness of his dark gaze. 'I've finished my thesis and it's been assessed. I'm working on my final portfolio. There's an exhibition for Masters students held at one of the galleries. It's a chance to get noticed by the art world.'

'You have enjoyed the course?' he asked.

'Yes, very much,' she answered. 'It's all I've ever wanted to do.'

'Are your parents a little more resigned to your career choice?'

She gave him a grim look. 'I think you know enough about my parents to know they would have preferred me to be doing something a little less controversial.'

'Controversial?' His brow creased slightly. 'What is controversial about being an artist?'

'You obviously haven't seen any of my recent work,' she said with a wry grimace.

His dark eyes twinkled. 'So you have been milking some very sacred cows have you, *cara*?'

'That's not quite the expression I would have chosen but I guess it will do,' she conceded. 'I painted a rather subversive political work. It caused a bit of furore.'

'With your father or the public?'

'Both,' she said. 'I was at a demonstration and took it with me. I'm surprised you didn't hear about it in the press.'

'I must have been interstate or overseas at the time,' he said, frowning slightly. 'Were you arrested?'

'Not this time,' she said. 'But my father threatened to disinherit me if it happened again.'

Patrizio examined her features for a lengthy moment. 'Our separation has not helped your relationship with your parents, has it?' he asked.

She shook her head and began toying with the meal the waiter had set before her moments earlier. 'No…but then that's my fault and I accept total responsibility for it.'

Patrizio wondered if she really had. She seemed intent on sticking to her story of not remembering that night, which annoyed him immensely. She had wilfully gone to Merrick's flat with the intention of resuming her relationship with him. There was no point in pretending she didn't know how she'd ended up in bed with him. She couldn't have chosen a more lethal blow to their marriage than that.

'You do not look like you are enjoying your meal,' he remarked. 'Did I choose the wrong thing for you?'

She shook her head and put her cutlery down. 'No, I guess I'm not as hungry as I thought. My appetite is still not back to normal since I had that bug.'

'Come,' he said, pulling her to her feet. 'We have achieved what we set out to achieve. The press has got their statement from us. We will go home.'

'But what about your meal?' Keira asked. 'Aren't you going to finish it?'

He handed her his handkerchief, his expression wry. 'I seem to have lost my appetite as well,' he said. 'Besides, it has been a long day. I am ready for bed.'

Bed.

One word.

Three letters.

Keira shivered as his arm came around her waist as he led her from the restaurant.

If trying to get through a meal with him had been hard, what on earth was it going to be like spending the next six weeks lying in his bed beside him?

CHAPTER FIVE

'I HAVE some emails to see to on the computer in my office,' Patrizio informed Keira once they had returned to his house. 'I will leave you to prepare for bed. I will try not to disturb you when I join you later.'

She swallowed. 'Which side do you want me to sleep on?'

His eyes hardened slightly as they meshed with hers. 'What is your preference these days?' he asked. 'Right or left, or do you still lie right in the middle?' *Sprawled like a whore*, he added silently, his gut twisting all over again with the venomous vipers of jealousy.

'I don't have a preference.'

His top lip lifted sardonically. 'Then perhaps we should toss a coin.' He took one out of his trouser pocket and started turning it over in his hand. 'Your call. Heads is the right side, tails is left.'

'Heads,' she said, feeling her stomach trip over itself in apprehension.

He tossed the coin and, deftly catching it, turned over his hand to show her. 'You lose.'

Yet again, Keira thought. She had never won anything when it came to a contest with Patrizio. He had an innate ability to turn things to his advantage. Even their bitter break up—splashed all over the newspapers as it had been—had generated a huge groundswell of public support for him, taking his business to the heights of success. Shares in the company had doubled overnight, investors had clamoured to get on board, property developers wanted his and only his luxury home designs for their new estates. He had made millions out of her betrayal and, in spite of his obvious bitterness and anger towards her, she couldn't help feeling he had probably been laughing all the way to the bank ever since.

'Goodnight, Keira,' he said into the pulsing silence.

She turned away without answering, her shoulders going down as her legs carried her upwards.

Patrizio tore his gaze away from her passage up the stairs, his jaw rigid as he clenched and unclenched his fists until his fingers ached.

Six weeks.

It wasn't long. He could do it. He could lie next to her for forty-five nights without touching her.

He *had* to do it.

Keira had the dream again. She hadn't had it for several weeks but it was just as terrifyingly real as the last time.

She shot upright in bed, her chest heaving in panic, her heart racing as the sound of her scream still reverberated off the walls.

'What the hell?' Patrizio woke with a start, his pupils instantly shrinking as Keira turned on the bedside lamp.

'Sorry…' she mumbled as she got out of bed, hugging her arms across her chest, her oversized pyjamas making her look more like a child than a woman of close to twenty-five.

'Did you have a nightmare or something?' he asked.

She rubbed her hands up and down her arms. 'I didn't mean to wake you…I had a bad dream…Sorry…'

He flung the bedcovers aside and went to where she was standing, her body still visibly trembling. He touched her on the shoulder and felt her flinch, her body shrinking away from him. He let his hand fall and sent it on a rough pathway through his hair instead. 'Would you like a drink of water or something?' he offered.

She gave a little shudder and turned to face him, her eyes meeting his briefly before slipping away again. 'Yes…that would be good…thanks…'

Patrizio was glad of an excuse to leave the room while he got his reaction to her vulnerability under some sort of control. Surely she had never been this fragile before. It got to him. It *really* got to him. It made him want to protect her, to hold her close and soothe away her fears as he had done so often in the past.

Fool, he reprimanded himself. She was probably doing it deliberately. The divorce settlement wasn't going her way, he had been making it as difficult as he could and she was no doubt using this brief reconciliation to her advantage, making him desire her all over again so he would agree to her outrageous demands.

He'd have to watch himself around her. She was a temptress. She had always had that look of little-girl-lost innocence about her. She had claimed to be a virgin when he'd first met her but now, with hindsight, he seriously doubted it. She had slept with him on that first night without hesitation. He had fallen in love with her when she told him he had been her first lover. It had knocked him sideways to think she had waited when so many young women of her age had numerous notches on their belts. He had been blinded by lust and the dream of having her exclusively to himself. He had married her as quickly as he could, never once realising that she still held a candle for her childhood sweetheart, Garth Merrick.

And if it hadn't been for Bruno's and Jamie's education hanging in the balance he would be free of her by now.

God, how he wanted to be free of her!

She was temptation in a five foot seven package that he didn't want to unwrap again.

It wasn't Jamie's fault that his older sister was a tramp. He was a good kid, a bit introverted and uncertain of himself, which made Bruno's bullying towards him all the harder to excuse.

When he thought about it, his nephew had been a time bomb waiting to detonate. The loss of his father at the age of seven had knocked him off course; it had knocked them all off course. Patrizio had done his best but it clearly hadn't been enough.

He sighed as he filled a glass with water and carried it back upstairs. Bruno was still hurting and that hurt was being played out with this totally uncharacteristic bullying behaviour. It was now up to him to set an example for his nephew, one of forgiveness and reconciliation, in public at least, even if he couldn't quite manage to pull it off in private. It would be difficult but worth it if the boys were able to resolve their differences and move on with their lives.

Keira sat on the edge of the bed, her hands clasped in her lap as she tried to regroup. She was back in Patrizio's life, acting as if things were normal, when nothing but acrimony bubbled like scalding lava between them. It didn't help that she still loved him. That was what made her betrayal of him all the harder to understand. She had been angry—yes, and hurt to think he might have been sleeping around—but she had never dreamt of doing the same thing and certainly not with Garth, who had been the closest friend she'd ever had. In all the years she had known him, she had never felt anything but sisterly affection for him, which made it all the more inexcusable that she had acted as she had.

If only she could remember the details of that night! She had gone to Garth's flat, beside herself with distress, a migraine already boring a hole behind her right eye from all the weeping she had done. He had gathered her close just like he had done for most of their lives, telling her it would sort itself out. He had offered her a glass of wine, which she had sipped in between sobs in an effort to calm herself. But after a while she had put the glass to one side as her headache had worsened. She had been wretchedly sick and sobbed some more before collapsing into bed, not even caring that it was the only one in the flat. Besides, they'd shared a bath together many times when they were little kids; it was like sleeping with a relative…or so she had thought…

She had sat up that morning, her pupils still protesting at the blindingly bright light coming in through the chink in the curtains. 'Garth?' she croaked and then, looking down at her nakedness, clutched at the tangled sheet near her feet and wrenched it upwards to cover herself as he came in.

'How's your head?' he asked, handing her a glass of chilled water.

She took it with unsteady hands. 'What happened last night?' she asked, not really sure she wanted to know. 'I don't remember anything past me arriving with a headache and telling you about…about…' she could barely say the words without feeling the pain of them scoring her throat '…Patrizio's affair.'

He avoided her gaze, a dull flush running underneath the skin of his cheeks. 'We slept together,' he said.

Her eyes widened in spite of the pain it caused her. 'You mean as in *slept together?*'

He gave her a brief nod, the line of his mouth grim.

Her chest felt as if it were going to collapse inwards under the weight of her guilt and shame. 'Oh, my God…' she gasped in shock. 'What have I done? Oh, God…no. *No!* I couldn't possibly have…'

'It's all right, Keira,' he said. 'We didn't do anything wrong. Lots of friends sleep together. It's not a big deal these days.'

Keira stared at him in horror, unable to believe she had acted so impulsively, so out of control, so recklessly and shamefully. 'I—I don't know what to say…I'm so ashamed to have…to have led you on like that…' She swallowed and looked at him again. 'Did I have too much to drink or something? I only remember drinking half a glass. I'm always so careful with alcohol, you know I am…'

He got off the bed, his indrawn breath striking a chord of unease inside her. 'Your husband saw you,' he said. 'He came here this morning, a couple of hours ago. I didn't want to let him in but he barged through before I could stop him. The press was here as well. I think some of them are still waiting outside. You'd better not leave until they clear off.'

Keira's distress at hearing that rendered her speechless.

Garth turned around to look at her. 'It was the best thing that could have happened, Keira. After all, he's been doing the dirty on you. Why shouldn't you do it to him? Talk about double standards. I don't see why you should be feeling so guilty. It wasn't your fault.'

It didn't excuse her. Nothing could do that. She had slept with another man and Patrizio had every right to be angry.

He would never forgive her, any more than she could forgive herself.

Patrizio handed her the glass of water, watching as her eyes carefully avoided his as their fingers met briefly. He felt the lightning bolt of awareness zap him the way it always had, the sensual heat of her body coming towards him drawing him in like a powerful magnet did to an iron filing. Desire surged in his lower body, the blood roaring through him as he remembered the way her body had writhed and twisted beneath the desperate thrusting and plunging of his.

He had buried himself in several women since in an effort to expunge her from his memory, but not one of them had taken him to the unbelievable heights of pleasure he had experienced in Keira's arms.

'I'm sorry I woke you,' she said again, her soft voice pushing against the silence.

'It's all right,' he said, pulling back the sheets to get back in. 'I was half awake, anyway.'

He felt the depression of the mattress as she lay back down; he could even feel the warmth of her body even though she was as far away from him as the king-sized bed allowed.

The silence crawled like an invisible entity from every corner of the room and even the numbers on the digital bedside clock seemed too bright once the lamp was switched off.

'I forgot to ring my parents,' she said after five minutes had passed.

'Will they worry if you do not answer your phone at your flat?' he asked.

He heard the rustle of the bedclothes as she shifted position. 'Probably not,' she answered with an almost inaudible sigh.

'What about your mobile phone? Do you have it with you?'

'No, I dropped it a few weeks ago and it broke. I haven't replaced it,' she said. 'Anyway, I couldn't afford the bills.'

Patrizio frowned in the darkness. She was no doubt trying to make him feel guilty about not agreeing to pay her generous amounts of alimony, but he wasn't going to budge.

He wasn't handing over half of his wealth to his sluttish ex-wife, who would no doubt share it with her lover.

'I will organise a mobile phone for you tomorrow,' he said. 'I will see to the bills until we bring our reconciliation to its inevitable end.'

She didn't say anything and for a few minutes he wondered if she had fallen asleep but then she said, 'My parents are going to get an awful shock when they read tomorrow's paper.'

'Yes…I guess they will.'

The sheets rustled again.

'Patrizio?'

'Mmm?'

'I really regret how things turned out,' she said, her voice sounding husky. 'We had it all going for us and I threw it away…I can't believe I was so stupid.'

'We all make mistakes,' he said on the back of a heavy sigh. 'It's over, Keira. We have to move on.'

He felt her turn on the mattress to face him; he could even feel the soft waft of her breath on his face and mouth when she spoke.

'Do you think you will ever be able to forgive me?' she asked in a soft pleading whisper.

'Go to sleep, Keira,' he said, rolling over to face the wall. 'This is not the time to talk of forgiveness.'

'Is there ever going to be a time?' she asked after another strung-out silence.

He lifted his head and punched his pillow into shape before answering, keeping his tone detached and emotionless. 'Probably not. Now, for God's sake go to sleep.'

Keira blinked back tears and turned to face the wall on her side. 'Goodnight, Patrizio,' she said in a soft whisper.

He didn't answer but within minutes she heard the even sound of his breathing which indicated he had fallen asleep.

I should be so lucky, she thought and, sighing, turned over and stared blankly at the ceiling.

Keira woke to the warmth of Patrizio's body lying spoon-like against her back and his hand on her breast, the caressing movement against her nipple stirring her into instant tingling awareness. Heat coursed through her as she felt the probe of his aroused length nudge at the back of her thighs, the satin-covered steel as it instinctively sought her liquid warmth making her stomach instantly somersault.

'P-Patrizio?'

'Mmm?' He began to nuzzle her neck, his tongue snaking out to blaze a hot moist trail to the shell of her ear.

'We're...we're not supposed to be doing this...' she said, shivering in reaction as his thumb and forefinger pressed her nipple in a gentle but totally tantalising pinch.

'You are on my side of the bed,' he said, the pulsing heat of him locking her breath high up in her throat. 'I can only assume that is because you want me to make love to you.'

She would have denied it but two of his long fingers had already found the silky wet evidence for themselves, the smooth glide of them within her ridged tightness shocking her, arching her spine and curling her toes.

'You are so hot and ready for me,' he growled deep in his throat. 'I would only have to roll you over and sink into you to prove how much of a wanton you really are.'

Keira stiffened at his words, shame rushing through her all over again. Was this how it had happened between her and Garth that night? Had she been so easy, so willing and available that she hadn't even realised who was caressing her until it was too late?

'But I am not going to do it,' Patrizio said, moving away from her. 'I am not going to taint myself with soiled goods.'

Keira squeezed her eyes shut, the pain of his rejection hurting far more than it should have done under the circumstances. She had known all along he no longer loved her. Why then should she be feeling this crushing pain right in the middle of her chest?

CHAPTER SIX

MORNINGS were not Keira's favourite time of the day—they never had been. Her mother had spent most of Keira's childhood threatening her with cupfuls of ice to get her out of bed for school but it had rarely worked. There was something about lying cocooned in a soft-as-a-feather quilt that fulfilled Keira's most primal yearnings. She hated leaving that comforting warmth to face the day, knowing that as soon as she left that haven of peace everything that could go wrong would go wrong and make her long to dive back in and hide from the world all over again.

'Are you going to get up or lie in there all day?' Patrizio asked as he positioned the knot of his tie into place in front of the mirror near the bed.

Keira pulled the covers back over her head. 'I don't have to go to college today.'

'Lucky for some,' he said, reaching for his jacket and keys.

She peeped over the edge of the covers to look at him. 'Is there anything you want me to do while you're at work?' she asked.

He shrugged himself into his jacket. 'Nothing but for you to continue to play the role of devoted wife with whomever you come into contact,' he said. 'Don't forget Marietta is watching your every move.' He checked his watch and added, 'If you're feeling up to it, I have a trade function tonight that will give more credibility to our reconciliation. The press will be there in droves.'

'I don't have anything to wear,' she said, desperately looking for a way out.

Patrizio raised his eyes heavenwards and reached for his wallet and peeled off a wad of notes and placed them on the bed. 'Go and buy yourself something,' he said. 'And make it sexy and glamorous. I don't want you to turn up looking like a cash-strapped arts student, otherwise people will wonder why on earth I have taken you back.'

Keira felt like poking her tongue out at him. 'I wouldn't be cash-strapped if you'd agreed to the terms of the settlement,' she threw at him petulantly.

His dark eyes glinted as they caught and held hers. 'You never know, *cara*, I might well give you what you are asking for if you behave yourself for the next six weeks.'

She snorted and dived under the covers again. 'Go to hell.'

'Your father phoned, by the way.'

Her head came back out, her violet-blue eyes instantly wary. 'What did he say?'

'He wanted to know if we were genuine about being together again. I don't think he found the short article in the paper all that convincing.'

'What did you say?'

His mouth tilted wryly. 'What do you think I said?'

'It was probably something along the lines of, "I am doing this for the sake of the boys' education or for the sake of my adopted country" or something nauseatingly altruistic like that,' she said with a hint of pique.

He raised one dark brow. 'You do not think protecting the boys is a worthwhile enterprise?'

She had no choice but to back down. 'Of course I think it's worth it, I just don't like being caught up in the middle of it all.'

He snatched up his keys and phone. 'You wouldn't have been caught in the middle of it if you hadn't been caught in another man's bed. Perhaps you should think about *that* today in the absence of other intellectual stimulation.'

Keira wanted the last word but he didn't give her time to deliver it. The door had slammed on his exit before she had even opened her mouth.

She let out a defeated sigh and, flopping back down, threw the covers back over her head.

Hunger was the only thing that lured her out a couple of hours later. She showered and, finger-combing her hair, ventured into the kitchen where Marietta was bustling about emptying the dishwasher and wiping down the already spotlessly clean benches.

'Ah, you are finally awake!' she said with a knowing grin. 'No doubt that sexy husband of yours kept you busy all night, eh?'

Keira felt the colour rise up from her feet to pool into her cheeks. 'Er…yes…' she said, smiling uncomfortably.

Marietta winked. 'You need a quiet day, yes? You will be sore if you do not rest properly. You will not be ready for him tonight if you do not take it easy.'

Keira felt like a fraud and hated herself all over again for deceiving the housekeeper, who clearly had high hopes for a long and happy reunion between her boss and his wayward wife.

Marietta came closer and patted her on the arm. 'Listen to me; I am much older than you but I know a lot of things about men. Your husband is like a lot of Italian men. He does not like to share. But he has women after him all the time, no? Why should you stay at home and feel bad, eh? You make him a little bit jealous but what about how he makes you feel, huh? I see the papers, I hear the rumours. He is a very rich man and lots of women want him. You made a mistake but who doesn't, eh? Put it behind you and move on. That is my advice.'

'Thank you, Marietta,' she said. 'I am doing my best to move on.'

Marietta smiled. 'You love him. I can see that. You did not stop loving him. That is why I kept your clothes in the wardrobe. I knew you would come back. It is where you belong, no?'

'No…I mean yes…it's where I belong,' Keira said, inwardly sighing as she thought about the next few weeks living as Patrizio's wife under the watchful eye of his housekeeper.

Keira's mother phoned just as she was leaving the house to go shopping for an outfit. Marietta brought the phone to her and left her in privacy in the lounge overlooking the muddy brown water of the Yarra River.

'Is it true, Keira?' Robyn asked. 'Are you really reunited with Patrizio?'

'Yes, it's true,' she said, for some reason not feeling so guilty about lying to her mother. 'The divorce is off.'

She heard her mother's long drawn out sigh of relief. 'Thank God you've come to your senses at last. I had a feeling once you and Patrizio came face to face you would both realise what you were throwing away. You injured his pride in the most despic—'

'Mum, please.' Keira cut her off quickly. 'Lecturing me about the past is not going to help us now. We're making a fresh start and we'd appreciate it if you would cooperate by not mentioning what happened ever again. I made a mistake. It could easily have been the other way around, you know.'

'But it wasn't,' her mother said. 'Patrizio meant his wedding vows when he made them. I have never seen a man more in love with a woman than he was with you. It grieves me to think of how you have hurt him after all he's done for us.'

Keira's hand tightened around the phone. 'What do you mean, "after all he's done for us"? What are you talking about?'

'I...nothing,' Robyn said. 'I just meant he's been very nice about it all, not involving your father and me and James in his bitterness towards you. He has always remained pleasant and friendly towards us.'

'When have you seen him?' Keira asked, suspicion starting to crawl all over her skin like an insect. 'Have you been in regular contact with him over the past two months?'

'We saw no reason not to see him occasionally,' Robyn answered. 'Of course we didn't tell you about it, knowing it would only cause another one of your childish scenes.'

Keira wasn't sure how to deal with this revelation. She had not for a moment realised that Patrizio had kept in such close contact with her family. She knew he had always been fond of Jamie, and he had always been polite towards her parents, but when their divorce was weeks away from being finalised it seemed odd that he would have encouraged such a connection, even if it had only been occasional.

'I hope this time around you are going to be a good wife to him, Keira,' her mother said, filling the small silence. 'And I also hope you are not going to see Garth again. His mother told me he's seeing a nice girl who is visiting from Canada. She hasn't met her yet but I would hate to think—'

'Mum, I haven't seen Garth for weeks,' she said. 'I'm happy for him if he's found someone. He deserves to be happy.'

Her mother gave another heartfelt sigh of relief. 'Well, then,' she said, 'I'd better go. I have to attend a pre-selection function with your father this evening. I must say your reconciliation with Patrizio came at a very good time. Your father's chance of re-election to the Senate for another term will be boosted by the news of his family life being back on track.'

Keira felt like rolling her eyes. Appearances were everything to her parents; their whole lives revolved around doing the right thing at the right time, speaking to the right people, wearing the right clothes, eating at the right restaurants, reading the right books and newspapers, even listening to the right television and radio stations. She hated it all. It all seemed so shallow and false. She would much rather speak to some of the homeless people she walked past on her way to art school every day. At least their smiles when she bought them a sandwich or a coffee were genuine.

The boutique Keira chose was not a particularly up-market one but it had a magnolia-white satin dress that appealed to her instantly. It skimmed her curves in all the right places, the cutaway back showing off the pale skin of her spine almost to her buttocks. The front was equally daring, the plunging neckline requiring tape to keep her breasts from spilling out. Patrizio had wanted sexy and glamorous and he was going to get it, she thought as she waited for the cashier to wrap it in tissue paper.

Next was a trip to the cosmetic section of one of the larger department stores, where an attendant expertly applied a natural-looking foundation to Keira's face, before highlighting the unusual blue of her eyes with smoky eye-shadow and eyeliner.

Her hair was soon dealt with at a plush salon in the Southgate section of the Southbank complex that ran along the Yarra River.

An hour later Keira couldn't believe how different she looked. Her curly dark hair was scooped on top of her head, one loose tendril falling over her right eye, giving her a come-and-get-me look.

Even the cab driver kept looking at her in the rear-view mirror. 'Going somewhere special this evening?' he asked.

'Yes, to a function with my husband.'

'Lucky man,' he said and, glancing at her again, commented, 'You look kind of familiar. Weren't you in the paper this morning?'

'Er…yes,' she said, smiling stiffly. She hadn't intended to look at the article but, while she had been waiting for her hairdresser to finish with another client, she had flicked through the paper lying on the counter next to her. It hadn't been too bad a photo all things considered. She looked like a woman very much in love with her husband and Patrizio had looked as devastatingly handsome as usual, his adoring smile giving no clue to the animosity he felt for her.

'You're Patrizio Trelini's wife, aren't you?' the cab driver said. 'My brother-in-law works in the building industry. Trelini Luxury Homes, right?'

'Yes…'

'He's close to being a billionaire now, huh?' he went on. 'Gotta admire him, starting out with virtually nothing and building up an empire like that. That's what this country needs, more men like that. Not afraid of a bit of hard work.'

'Yes…'

'So you're back together again, huh?' he said, his eyes holding hers a little too long.

'Yes, that's right.'

'He's a better man than me, then,' he said as he pulled up in front of Patrizio's house. 'I wouldn't take back my wife if she slept around. No way.'

Keira tightened her mouth. 'How much do I owe you?' she asked.

He told her and she handed him a fifty-dollar bill. 'Keep the change,' she said, and scooping up her bags, left with the colour of her shame flooding her cheeks.

CHAPTER SEVEN

KEIRA was bending towards the mirror in the *en suite* bathroom reapplying her lipstick when Patrizio came home. He stepped into the room behind her, stopping in his tracks momentarily as his gaze swept over her.

She turned around to look at him, her chin tilted at a defiant angle. 'How do I look?' she asked.

Patrizio could barely breathe with her delectable body so close. The delicate but intoxicating fragrance of her perfume made his nostrils instantly flare, the tempting shadow of her cleavage in her low-cut gown making his hands ache to reach out and free her breasts from the silky fabric that was defying all odds to keep them covered. She surely couldn't be wearing any underwear beneath that dress; there wasn't a line in sight, just smooth uninterrupted alluring curves. The thought of her, totally naked beneath that length of silk, made his groin spring to life, hot surging blood filling him with a need so strong he wondered if she could smell the musky male scent of arousal coming off him. He could lift that dress right this minute and sink inside her; the temptation to do so was almost unbearable.

'You look very beautiful,' he said, stripping his voice of all emotion. 'Give me ten minutes to shower and shave and change into my tuxedo and we will get going. I have organised for someone to drive us. I don't want to be bothered with parking in the city.'

'I'll wait for you in the lounge,' she said, brushing past him.

He clenched his fists once she had gone, his teeth grinding together as he faced his reflection in the mirror. *'Only a fool makes the same mistake twice,'* he reminded himself harshly. *'Do not forget that.'*

The stretch limousine arrived just as Patrizio joined Keira in the lounge and he ushered her outside with a hand cupping her elbow, reminding her in a low tone that they had a role to play.

'I haven't forgotten,' she said, flashing him a little glance of annoyance.

His fingers tightened around her elbow. 'Drivers have ears and eyes, *cara*,' he cautioned her.

Keira got in the car with a forced smile on her face, her breath sucking in sharply when Patrizio slid along the seat to reach for her hand, placing it on the long muscular length of his thigh.

She swallowed as he moved her hand to rest between his thighs where his body was already stirring. She felt the rise of his flesh beneath the pads of her fingertips, her stomach stumbling over the trip-wire of instantaneous desire that raged through her like a flash flood of fire.

His eyes met hers, the glitter of rampant desire in his coal-black gaze making her spine feel as if it had been unhinged, vertebrae by vertebrae. Her mouth went dry as one of his fingers traced a scorching pathway from the base of her neck, past her breasts, skating over each ripe curve that peeped out tantalisingly.

'You are not wearing anything under that dress, are you, Keira?' he asked in a husky low voice.

'Two bits of tape,' she said, running her tongue over her lips. 'That's all.'

His mouth curved upwards in a smile that didn't seem to her to be entirely genuine. 'Did you do it deliberately to tempt me?' he asked.

Keira glanced towards the driver's compartment but the glass partition was shut, and she hoped, totally soundproof. 'No, of course not. You told me to dress sexily and glamorously and I followed your orders. That's what I'm supposed to do, isn't it? Follow your orders to a T.'

'That is correct,' he said, removing her hand to place it back on his thigh. 'As long as you do as you are told we will get through this with ease.'

The function centre was packed with guests when they arrived, every head turning as they entered the room. Keira knew what everyone was thinking. She could see it in their eyes each time they met hers.

Harlot.

Jezebel.

Tramp.

Whore.

The double standard sickened her. She knew a considerable proportion of the married men in the room would have cheated on their wives at one time or another. Sociological research statistics proved it, but it was an entirely different story when a woman was unfaithful.

The press had hounded her relentlessly in the last two months; their large black lenses of accusation aimed at her at every opportunity. And as they surged towards her now she felt herself shrinking inside, as if someone were stitching her belly button to her backbone.

Cameras flashed almost constantly and her face started to

ache within minutes from smiling and being polite to everyone who came over to speak to her.

Just when she thought she could stand it no longer, she caught sight of a familiar face. Melissa was married to Leon Garrison, one of Patrizio's chief architects. Melissa worked as an interior designer and had often stopped to chat to Keira in the past, although recently she had been away on maternity leave.

'Wow, how nice to see you again, Keira,' she said. 'I was so thrilled to hear you and Patrizio are back together.'

'Thank you,' Keira answered, hoping she wasn't looking as hot on the outside as she felt on the inside.

'I heard about what happened,' Melissa said, edging her over to a quiet corner. 'I mean about that incident with Rita Favore.'

Keira bit her lip. 'Oh…'

'She's a total man-eating cow,' Melissa said. 'She made a play for my husband as well. She sent a saucy message to his phone but luckily I saw through it.'

'I should have realised…'

'Don't be too hard on yourself,' Melissa said. 'Patrizio's obviously forgiven you now and that's all that matters. I really felt for you when the press were making all those horrible comments about you all the time. They just don't let up, do they? It's totally unfair. Boys will be boys but, for some reason, women are still supposed to be pure as the driven snow.'

'I would give anything to change what happened,' Keira said. 'The worst part is I don't even remember doing it.'

Melissa's eyes went wide. 'What do you mean?'

Keira rolled her lips together for a moment as she tried as she had done so many times before to piece together that night. 'I had the most appalling scene with Patrizio,' she said.

'I didn't listen to his explanations of what the Favore woman had done; instead I demanded a divorce, I think more to make him stand up and take notice. I was feeling a bit neglected as he'd been away such a lot but it sort of backfired. I left in tears and ended up driving around for hours until I came to a friend's house. He gave me a glass of wine to calm me down. I was sure I only had half a glass but I can't really remember anything so maybe I had more than I realised…'

'Yeah, well, drinking too much alcohol can certainly do that,' Melissa said. 'A friend of mine got so drunk after a night on the town she didn't remember where she'd been for over four hours. She woke up in bed at home and couldn't even recall how she got there. Scary, huh?'

'Tell me about it,' Keira said with a rueful grimace. 'If I hadn't seen the evidence for myself I would never have believed I had slept with Garth. He's been like a brother to me ever since we were little toddlers playing in the sandpit at pre-school.'

'You mean there was absolutely no doubt you had slept with him?' Melissa asked.

Keira looked at her for a stretching moment, wondering if Garth had lied to her. But why would he? What possible motivation could he have had? He had been her closest friend since childhood, their mothers were best friends and their fathers were in the same family-focused conservative political party. Garth would never have lied about something that would have such devastating consequences for her. Her life had been in ruins ever since that night; there was no way he would allow that to continue if they hadn't actually done what he had said they had done.

'There's no doubt,' she said with a sigh. 'No doubt at all.'

'Well, as I said, it's in the past so forget about it and enjoy this second chance with Patrizio,' Melissa said and, swinging her gaze to take in the hubbub of the room, added, 'God, I hate these functions, don't you? My feet are killing me in these heels.'

'Mine too.' Keira smiled, warming to the young woman's open friendliness. She had missed female companionship over the last two months. Her few friends had shunned her as the news of her betrayal had spread, and the constant press attention certainly hadn't helped the situation. No one wanted to be seen with her in case they were documented as socialising with a slut. She had become a bit of hermit as a result, concentrating on completing her studies and doing her level best to survive each gruelling day.

But it had taken its toll. Even now she was feeling the lead weights of weariness begin to drag at her legs, her stomach grumbling with the faint queasiness that lately never seemed to go away.

'I'd better get back to Leon,' Melissa said. 'How about we meet up for lunch some time? I'd love to show you little Samuel. He's six weeks old. My mum's minding him tonight. It's the first time I've left him. My breasts are threatening to burst and I've only been here thirty minutes.'

'I'd love to see him,' Keira said, suppressing the deep pang of longing that assailed her at the thought of a tiny baby nuzzling her own breasts. She had dreamed of starting a family with Patrizio; she had even discussed names with him before they had parted so acrimoniously.

'I'll give you a call in the next week,' Melissa said. 'It was wonderful to chat with you. I've missed seeing you around.'

'Thank you,' she said shyly. 'I've missed seeing you too.'

Patrizio came back over just after Melissa rejoined her husband. 'Sorry to leave you for so long,' he said, his hand settling on the curve of her hip in a possessive manner. 'I got cornered by one of the advertising executives.'

'That's OK,' she said, her skin lifting at the feel of his

touch, with just a thin layer of silk separating his hand from her body. 'I enjoyed seeing Melissa again. I didn't visit her when she had the baby.'

'Why not?'

'I was worried I might run into you…'

'So you put your feelings ahead of your friend's?' he asked. 'Not very loyal of you, was it?'

Keira couldn't hold his gaze. She bit her lip and looked down at her purse, her knuckles going white as pain ripped through her. She felt him watching her, the heat of his gaze burning through the thin layer of her clothes. Tears stung her eyes but she forced them back. She had a role to play and she was going to play it.

'Would you like a fresh drink?' Patrizio asked as a waiter drifted towards them.

She shook her head and handed him her barely touched glass of orange juice. 'No, I'm just going to the ladies' room. Excuse me.'

He watched her walk away; every eye turned to look as she left the room, the speculative glances enough to unsettle the strongest of personalities.

He let out a sigh and turned to face one of the sales staff who had called out to him.

Six weeks, he reminded himself as the man began speaking, not a word of which he could recall less than ten minutes later.

Six weeks.

Keira locked herself in one of the cubicles and took some deep calming breaths. She heard other women come and go, their idle chatter barely registering as she tried to concentrate on keeping a lid on her emotions.

'Gosh, Patrizio Trelini's wife is gorgeous, don't you

think?' A woman's voice suddenly broke through Keira's consciousness.

'Sure is,' another woman replied. 'No wonder he's decided to take her back. Mind you, I don't know what all the fuss was about in the first place. It's not as if he hasn't had the odd fling. I wonder what his current mistress thinks of him going back to his wife, or maybe he's going to have his bit on the side as a sort of payback.'

'Wouldn't surprise me,' the first woman said with a touch of cynicism. 'Besides, Gisela Hunter doesn't strike me as the type to move aside without a fuss.'

'Is she here tonight?'

'I saw her arrive just before we came in here,' the other woman said. 'She was making a beeline for Patrizio. I wonder what the papers will make of that.'

'I wonder what his wife will make of that,' the first woman said wryly as they left.

Keira got to her feet and steeled her resolve with a gargantuan effort. She touched up her make-up and, taking another deep breath, went back out to the ballroom. She scanned the crowd for Patrizio's glossy black head that was usually at least three or four inches above everyone else's, but there was no sign of him.

'Are you looking for your husband?' the waiter who had served them earlier said on his way past with a tray of drinks.

'Yes…'

'I just saw him go through to the lounge area out there,' he said, pointing to the right.

Keira thanked him and made her way out to where he had directed, but it wasn't until she had moved past the lounge area to a small alcove behind a large arrangement of flowers that she saw him.

He was standing close to a tall blonde woman in her late

twenties, her close-fitting black dress showcasing her stunning figure in all the right places.

They were talking in hushed whispers. Keira couldn't make out what was being said but the body language between them was all she needed to see to know that his relationship with the woman was an intimate one.

She turned away, her heart contracting so suddenly that she thought she was going to faint. She stumbled back towards the ballroom and, weaving her way to the table they had been assigned, sat down and reached for her glass of water.

Gradually the rest of the tables filled and after about fifteen minutes Patrizio came and sat down beside her, his expression giving no hint of what Keira had witnessed.

'Cornered by another executive?' she asked with a pointed look.

'Yes,' he said, sending her a smile that didn't reach his eyes.

Keira silently seethed. She was sure the woman she had overheard in the ladies' room was right. He was doing it deliberately as a payback for what she had done. What better torture to dish out than to have her live and sleep with him for six weeks, knowing he was taking his pleasure elsewhere?

The meal was served but she barely touched it. She pushed each course as it was served around her plate, the occasional mouthful making it past her lips, but she tasted nothing but bitterness and regret.

A band began to play, which was a relief as it meant she no longer had to force herself to make conversation with the other guests at their table as the music was too loud to hear what anyone was saying with any accuracy.

Patrizio leaned towards her to speak directly against her ear. 'We should dance.'

'Should we?' she replied, her lips almost touching the cartilage of his ear.

He took her hand and pulled her to her feet before she could protest and led her to the dance floor, his arms going around her, bringing her in close to his pelvis as the band switched numbers to play a romantic ballad.

Keira had been prepared to dance a modern number with plenty of room between them, but having his body move in time with hers in a slow seductive dance was almost too much to bear. Her body betrayed her totally, her breasts tightened and peaked against the silk of her gown, her inner thighs moistened with the humid dew of desire and her lips began to tingle with the urge to feel his mouth pressing hard on hers.

'Relax, *cara*,' he said against her hair. 'You are like a broomstick.'

'Sorry…' She gave a little stumble but he steadied her by cupping her bottom with his hands.

'I had forgotten how well we fit together,' he said as they circled the dance floor. 'The top of your head fits just beneath my chin.'

'Only because I'm wearing heels.'

'We shall make a move to leave soon,' he said after they had weaved through the other couples who had joined them. 'I do not want you to have too late a night. We have another engagement tomorrow evening.'

She looked up at him in alarm. 'We do?'

'Take that worried look off your face,' he said in an undertone. 'Yes, I have organised to take the boys out for a meal. I have already cleared it with the headmaster.'

Keira felt her stomach go hollow. Jamie, of all people, would surely see through her thin façade. 'Won't your nephew object to being forced to spend the evening with Jamie, not to mention me?' she asked.

His hands fell away from her body to ensnare one of her hands as he led her from the dance floor. 'Bruno knows I expect him to behave with propriety, no matter what his feelings towards you or your brother are.'

'What about you?' she asked as they made their way to the waiting limousine. 'Will you behave with propriety or do you have a different set of rules for yourself?'

His black diamond gaze clashed with hers as he opened the door for her. 'Do not speak to me of rules, Keira,' he said in a clipped tone. 'After all, you are the one who doesn't know how to play by the rules.'

Keira bit back her retort when she heard other people spilling out of the hotel. Instead she got in the car, swishing her gown out of the way as he joined her on the seat.

She clenched her hands around her purse until her knuckles ached. She *had* to get control of her emotions. She knew it did her no favours where Patrizio was concerned. Losing her temper and sniping at him would only reinforce his opinion of her as a willful, unruly, unprincipled child. But it had hurt *so* much to see him huddled so companionably with that woman. Tears burned in her eyes but she blinked them back, focusing her attention on the strangled purse in her lap.

'The driver will take you home but I have to go back to my office to see to something urgent,' he said into the brittle silence a few minutes later. 'I am not sure what time I will be back.'

Keira swung her glittering blue gaze to his. 'I saw you talking to her,' she said. 'She's still your mistress, isn't she?'

He didn't bat an eyelid, she noticed, her resentment towards him burning deep and uncontrollably inside her.

'As of a few days ago she was—yes,' he responded smoothly. 'But in the interests of the boys I have temporarily suspended our involvement.'

Pain sliced through her, sharp unbearable pain that made her feel as if she were being taken apart piece by piece. No part of her was unaffected. She struggled to contain her reaction, every scrap of pride insisting she keep her voice even and controlled as if she didn't give a toss what he did or who he did it with.

'So after these six weeks are up you're going back to her?' she asked, forcing herself to meet that dark enigmatic gaze.

'That is the plan,' he said as the car drew to a halt outside his office tower.

Keira watched as he exited the car, his long strides taking him out of sight within a few seconds.

She sat back on the seat and laid her head back against the soft leather, her eyes tightly closed to keep back the bitter tears.

You have no right to be feeling so jealous, she reminded herself. You brought this on yourself and have no one else to blame.

No one but yourself…

CHAPTER EIGHT

KEIRA woke the next morning to find the bed had not been slept in on Patrizio's side. Her heart sank in despair as visions of him intimately entwined with Gisela Hunter filled her brain.

She threw off the bed covers and headed for the shower but even the scalding hot spray did nothing to ease the deep ache in her soul.

Marietta was bustling about the kitchen when Keira dragged herself downstairs with her art school backpack, which had arrived with the rest of her things the day before.

'Signor Trelini must have had a very early start, no?' the housekeeper said.

'Er…yes,' Keira said, glad she'd thought to ruffle the sheets on his side before she came downstairs.

'You want some breakfast? I have bacon and eggs and—'

'No, thank you, Marietta,' she said quickly as her stomach started to heave. 'I have to get to college. I have to finish some work for my final exhibition.'

Marietta peered at her. 'Are you feeling all right? You look very pale.'

Keira swallowed once or twice until the rolling waves of nausea stilled. 'I'm fine…really…I hate mornings. I never feel really human until about lunch time.'

'The separation, it was hard on you, no?' Marietta commented softly.

Keira felt tears rush to her eyes at the older woman's empathetic tone. 'Yes…yes it was but things are better now…'

'You are nearly finished your Masters degree, yes?'

'Yes,' Keira said with a relieved sigh. 'I just have to put the finishing touches to my portfolio of work and I'm done.'

'You are a very clever girl,' Marietta said. 'Me, I cannot draw a straight line.'

'My work is what you call abstract,' Keira explained. 'It's not to everyone's taste.' *Not my parents', in any case*, she tacked on mentally.

'Ah, but it is a gift to be able to translate your thoughts and feelings on to a canvas, is it not?'

'Yes, I guess so,' Keira said, recalling how her painting had been almost cathartic at times. 'But I don't think about what I'm feeling all the time; I just feel the urge to paint and I paint.'

'I feel the urge to cook,' the housekeeper said with a grin. 'But you are frustrating me for you do not eat. You are thinner than you used to be. You are not dieting, are you?'

'No, I just haven't been well for a few weeks,' she said. 'I got a bad stomach bug on top of the flu and haven't really picked up since.'

'You will be much better now you are back home,' Marietta said confidently. 'You were pining for him, no?'

'Yes, that's right,' Keira said, suddenly realising it was true. 'I was pining for him…"

Keira lost track of time in the studio at college. She had been allocated a small studio which she shared with another Masters student, who fortunately was not working that day, so it was a treat to be alone.

She looked at her watch after what had seemed to her to be only an hour to find that it was close to six p.m. She quickly cleaned her brushes and, locking up the studio, caught the next tram.

Patrizio was waiting for her when she arrived, his expression tight with anger. 'You are late,' he said and, running his eyes over her, added, 'and you are filthy.'

'I was working on my portfolio, I lost track of time.'

'You should have phoned.'

'There isn't a phone at the studio,' she said, starting to feel irritated by his tone.

'I have bought you a new mobile,' he said. 'It is charging in the kitchen. In future I would appreciate it if you would carry it at all times so you can let me know when you are going to be late.'

'You didn't come home at all last night and do you hear me bawling you out for not phoning to let me know what your arrangements were?' she threw at him crossly.

'You are not in a position to argue with me over my private arrangements,' he said with an imperious look.

'Your double standards make me sick,' she said. 'In spite of what you said to the contrary, you're continuing your affair with that woman to make me jealous.'

'Making you jealous would be a pointless exercise,' he put in coolly. 'You would have to be still in love with me for it to work, but you are not. You were not in love with me in the first place.'

'That's not true. I did love you.' *I do love you*, she silently added.

His lip curled in disdain. 'Your parents were right about you. They warned me you are wilful and disobedient, with a propensity for volatility and attention-seeking behaviour. I should have listened to them, not to mention some of my business associates who thought I was a fool for marrying you instead of just having a quick affair. They told me you were after my money but I stubbornly refused to listen.'

'Then why on earth did you marry me?' she tossed back. 'You could have just slept with me and saved yourself some hefty legal bills.'

His fists clenched by his sides, a nerve pulsing near his mouth, which was white-tipped with anger. 'That reminds me,' he said, reaching for an envelope and handing it to her. 'This came for you. It's from your lawyer.'

Keira took it from him with trembling fingers, glancing briefly at her lawyer's name and emblem on the left hand side of the envelope.

'Aren't you going to open it?' he asked after a short tense pause.

'Not right now,' she said, not sure that she wanted him to see what was documented there. Her lawyer, Rosemary Matheson, was a little on the ruthless side when it came to dealing with divorce settlements. Half the time Keira hadn't even listened to what Rosemary had said during their appointments. She'd usually sat picking at her cuticles, agreeing to whatever was suggested, hoping it would get Patrizio's attention and bring him storming back into her life.

'If you think for a moment that you are going to get half of my money, think again, Keira,' he said through lips pulled tight with anger. 'I will agree to a considerable payout but no way am I going to set you up for life after what you did to me. You duped me from the start.'

Keira looked up at him in confusion. 'What do you mean, I duped you from the start?'

'You led me to believe you were a virgin,' he said. 'I realise now, of course, that was all an act. You only told me that to reel me in to marry you.'

She stared at him open-mouthed. 'You think I *lied* about that?'

His eyes burned into hers. 'Didn't you?'

Her bottom lip began to tremble and she spun away so he wouldn't see it. 'No,' she said in a flat empty tone. 'You were my first lover.'

'But not your only one.'

She stiffened her spine and made her way to the stairs. 'I'm going to have a shower.'

'Keira.'

'I said I'm going to have a shower.' She kept moving, one foot after the other, knowing if she didn't get away from him right now he would see the devastation she was feeling.

She hadn't even heard him come up behind her. Suddenly she was on the landing with him holding her by the upper arms in an iron grip, his mouth thinned out with fury.

'You are determined to make me lose control, aren't you, Keira?' he asked. 'You want something to hold over me, some supposed misdemeanour that will make you feel less guilty about what you did.'

'No…' She struggled in his hold but he wouldn't release her. 'No, that's not true.'

'You are a wanton witch,' he ground out. 'You cannot live without a man in your bed. I see the hunger in your eyes. I saw it when you came to my office the other day. You are insatiable. One man was not enough for you. It is never going to be enough for you.'

She closed her eyes to shield herself from his hatred.

'Look at me, damn you!' he shouted, his fingers biting into her flesh.

Keira opened her eyes but by doing so opened the floodgates of her distress. She stood shaking in his hold, tears pouring from her eyes, sobs erupting from her throat with such brokenness that she felt her legs sway beneath her.

'Keira…' he said, his voice catching on her name. 'Do not do this. Why are you acting this way? It is not like you to cry at the drop of a hat.'

'P-please let me g-go…' she said between sobs.

Patrizio released her arms and brought her head down to his chest, one of his hands going to the nape of her neck. 'Shh,' he said, rocking her gently. 'Shh, *cara mio*.'

Keira snuggled against him, her anger towards him gradually abating as his tender caresses broke through her puny firewall of defences. She breathed in the clean male scent of him, her senses on full alert as his hand moved from her neck to her hair, his long fingers becoming entangled in her wild curls.

'I am not sure I can get through six weeks of this,' he said, his breath ruffling her hair. 'I thought I could, but now I'm not so sure.'

'Me too,' she whispered between noisy little sniffs. 'It's too hard…'

He tilted her chin up to look into her tear-washed blue eyes. 'I am perhaps not as immune to you as I thought,' he conceded grudgingly. 'My common sense says one thing but my body says another.'

She moistened the parched surface of her lips with the tip of her tongue. 'Mine too…'

'So what do we do about it?' he asked.

Keira held her breath, her eyes locked on his, her lower body throbbing against the surging heat of his. 'I don't know….' she said. 'Maybe ignore it and it will go away?'

He smiled lopsidedly. 'That is just so typical of you, Keira,' he said without any trace of malice in his tone. 'You do not like to face facts. You prefer to hide under the bed covers, yes?'

She felt a tiny wry smile tugging at her mouth at his accurate assessment of her character. 'I know, it's pathetic, isn't it? I should have well and truly grown out of the habit by now.'

He cupped her left cheek in the warmth of his hand. 'It is one of the things that made me fall in love with you. I do not think you should change.'

She looked at him with wide eyes; her heart suddenly seeming to need more space than it was currently allocated inside her chest. She watched as his mouth came down as if in slow motion, his breath briefly caressing the surface of her lips in that millisecond before the final touchdown.

As soon as his mouth covered hers, heat exploded in her belly. Flames of need licked and danced along her flesh until she was whimpering against the sensual assault of his mouth on hers. The first demanding thrust of his tongue rocked her to the core, liquid longing weeping from the walls of her femininity, the pulsing ache between her thighs almost unbearable.

His hands delved into her hair, holding her head as he deepened the kiss, his legs moving forwards against hers, making her step backwards until she was up against the wall.

She heard him groan with need as his hands left her hair to tear at her clothing, her loose-fitting cotton shirt popping every single button as he removed it from her. Her bra was next, the fastening barely undone before his mouth was sucking on each of her engorged nipples, his tongue rolling and curling until she was teetering on the edge of ecstasy.

He lifted his mouth from her breast to look into her eyes. 'You are the only person who can reduce me to this within seconds,' he said. 'I swore I would not touch you, but now that I have I do not want to stop.'

She clutched at him with desperate hands. 'I don't want you to stop. I want you to make love to me. I've missed you so much.'

'I cannot wait any longer to feel you again,' he said, lifting her skirt to cup her, his fingers moving aside the lacy barrier of her knickers to sink into her.

'Oh, God…' she groaned as his fingers rubbed against her intimately. 'Oh, please…*please*…'

He unzipped his trousers and released himself into her hands but he was too far gone for any preliminaries. After a brief moment he pushed her hands away and drove into her with a deep primal groan of satisfaction as her slippery warmth enclosed him tightly.

It was madness, it was far too rushed, it was reckless and almost savage, but it was unstoppable. Keira wondered if she was doing the right thing by agreeing to such intimacy between them while so much bitterness coloured their current relationship, but even as she rehearsed the words to slow things down her body had spun out of control.

Each urgent thrust took her higher and higher, her senses spinning as his mouth fed hungrily off hers. Her body sang with pleasure, every part of her responding to him with such instinctive fervour she could barely believe they had spent the last two months apart. Their bodies were still so in tune with each other, she knew him so intimately, and she knew exactly the moment when he was hovering on the edge of the precipice, his body tensing before the final devastating plunge into paradise.

She hadn't quite made the journey to the pinnacle of pleasure when she felt him lose control, his body pumping hard for a moment or two as his low and deep groan of release came out on a whoosh of warm breath that caressed her neck.

It was one of those moments Keira would have liked a little more time to prepare for. She had never known him to take his pleasure without ensuring her own first. She couldn't quite make up her mind if he had done it deliberately to imply she was nothing but a vessel for him to assuage his physical needs, or if he had genuinely lost control. She hoped it was the latter. Somehow that would make it easier to cope with.

'I am sorry,' he said, stepping back from her, his expression shuttered. 'That was not meant to happen.'

She lowered her eyes as she tried to cover herself, her emotions see-sawing all over again. 'It's all right… It was my fault just as much as yours…'

'Nevertheless I should not have allowed things to go that far,' he said as he rearranged his own clothing. 'I did not intend to make our reconciliation a physical one. This is not the way things are supposed to be between us. I don't want you to get the wrong idea, that's all.'

'I understand,' she said and turned for the bathroom rather than meet his eyes. 'I need to have a shower,' she added, her offhand tone belying the true state of her emotions. 'I'll try not to be too long.'

Patrizio raked a hand through his hair as he watched her leave, his skin still tingling from the contact with hers, the scent of her filling his nostrils until he felt as if he were breathing the very essence of her into his soul.

CHAPTER NINE

PATRIZIO was waiting for her as she came downstairs a short time later. She took each stair with deliberate care, frightened that she would take a tumble as that dark brooding gaze followed her progress.

'Keira,' he said, 'I think we need to talk through some things for a moment before we spend the evening in the boys' company.'

Keira pressed her lips together, not sure she wanted a post-mortem on what had happened earlier, so she disguised her feelings behind sarcasm. 'It wasn't a big deal, Patrizio,' she said. 'So you were a little trigger-happy. Maybe you need to sort that little problem out with your mistress. It's really nothing to do with me.'

'Damn it! It's everything to do with you!' he said. 'I do not know how to deal with you. One minute you are sobbing like a child in my arms, the next you are practically begging me to make love to you. I am at a loss to know which woman I am living with.'

Her eyes glittered as they met his. 'You're pretty good at sending out mixed messages yourself,' she threw back. 'I thought this was supposed to be a hands-off arrangement and here it is, day three, and you've had me up against the—'

'Do not make me sound like an animal.' He cut her off coldly, his jaw visibly tightening. 'You were with me all the way and you damn well know it.'

She gave him a little arch look. 'Not quite all the way,' she reminded him. 'You've certainly lost your touch, Patrizio.'

He ground his teeth and snatched up his keys from the hall table. 'You are nothing but a cheap little slut. I will be glad when this farce is over with. If it wasn't for the boys I would have been glad never to have seen or spoken to you again.'

'You and me too, baby,' she responded tartly.

He led the way to the car, his expression rigid with anger and his coal-black eyes flashing with wrath every time they clashed with hers.

They were well on their way to the boys' school when he finally broke the stiff silence. 'I hope I do not have to remind you of the importance of keeping our private feelings to ourselves. Jamie and Bruno are intelligent young men who will not be convinced of our reconciliation if we are shooting blistering looks at each other all evening.'

'You don't have to remind me,' she said. 'But it might help if you stop looking at me as if I've just recently crawled out from beneath a rock.'

His mouth twisted scathingly as he briefly met her gaze. 'I was thinking more along the lines of you recently crawling out of bed, but of course it's anyone's guess whose it might have been.'

She tightened her mouth. 'You're a two-faced bastard,' she said. 'You get quite a kick out of throwing all those stones from that glass house of yours, don't you?'

'I have had several lovers since we broke up,' he countered. 'I have not denied it.'

'And yet you think I'm a tramp for doing the same,' she said. 'That's totally sexist.'

'Just how many lovers have you had?' he asked as he parked the car in the staff car park.

Keira frowned as she recalled her previous statement. She had made it sound as if she'd been flitting from lover to lover when nothing could have been further from the truth.

'Having trouble recalling all their faces and names?' he asked when she didn't answer immediately.

'Patrizio, I…' she began, but just then she caught sight of her brother heading down the boarding house stairs with the housemaster, Mr Cartwright, and Bruno, Patrizio's nephew, lagging a few steps behind.

Patrizio sent her a warning look and got out of the car, shaking Mr Cartwright's hand before greeting both of the boys.

Keira hugged her brother, who patted her on the shoulder rather than fully return her embrace, but she could see the delight in his eyes.

She turned to the surly-looking boy standing near Patrizio and offered her hand. 'Hi, Bruno,' she said. 'How are you?'

'Fine,' he mumbled, barely touching her hand before shoving it back in his trouser pocket.

'Enjoy your evening,' Kent Cartwright addressed Keira and Patrizio and, turning to the boys, added soberly, 'Remember what we discussed earlier, gentlemen. If this problem is not sorted out, Mr Tinson will follow through on his threat to expel you both.'

'But that's not fair!' Jamie said, glaring at Bruno. '*He* started it.'

Bruno's lip curled insolently. '*You* started it by defending the behaviour of a common little sl—'

Patrizio cut him off with a curt command in Italian, before turning to the housemaster. 'My wife and I will sort this out, Mr Cartwright,' he said. 'We will have the boys back by ten p.m.'

Keira felt her skin tighten with shame at the searing glance Bruno sent her when Patrizio wasn't looking. She felt her face grow hot and her stomach began to churn as they got into the car. She didn't know how she was going to get through the evening; her emotions already felt scraped raw and they hadn't even left the school grounds.

'Anyway, I bet this is all an act,' Bruno said from the back seat once they were on their way.

'What do you mean by that, Bruno?' Patrizio asked, sending him a questioning glance in the rear-view mirror.

'You're not really back together,' he said sulkily.

'That is not true,' Patrizio said, reaching for Keira's hand and placing it on his thigh. 'We are very much together, aren't we, *cara*?'

Keira moistened the arid surface of her lips. 'Yes…' she said. 'Very much so.'

Bruno's tone was full of contempt. 'You said you'd never take her back, not after what she did. I wouldn't either. She's a filthy little—'

'Shut up, you idiot,' Jamie said.

Keira felt close to tears. 'Please, boys…don't do this…'

Patrizio glanced at her and, with a muttered curse, turned the car into the kerb. He took her into his arms and held her close. 'It is all right, *tesoro mio*,' he said, pressing a soft kiss to her forehead. 'You are not to take any notice of my nephew. He does not yet realise the depth of our love.'

She gave him a tremulous smile and took the handkerchief he offered, wishing with all her heart that he wasn't acting. 'I'm sorry…'

'No, you are not the one who should be apologising,' he said and, turning to his nephew, commanded, 'Bruno, you will apologise for insulting your aunt.'

'She's not my aunt,' Bruno said with another scowl.

'She is married to me and therefore is considered to be so,' Patrizio said.

'Yeah, well, how long is your marriage going to last?' Bruno said with another curl of his lip. 'You hardly made it to the first anniversary before she was—'

Patrizio let fly with a string of Italian that made Bruno clamp his lips together, but the look he sent Keira was still full of contempt.

The restaurant was thankfully close by, which meant the tension in the car lessened slightly with the change of scene.

Jamie came to Keira's side as they were led to their table, his expression concerned. 'Are you OK?'

She gave him a reassuring smile. 'I'm fine, Jamie. It's just all been a bit of an emotional roller coaster…you know…getting back together and all. I never thought it would happen.'

'Yeah, well, neither did I,' he said. 'But thank God it has. I've been so worried about you. Everyone has.'

Everyone apart from Patrizio, Keira thought. He would have been happier never to set eyes on her again but here he was, acting as if she were the love of his life.

'*Cara*, come and sit by me,' Patrizio said, taking her hand and leading her to the chair next to his.

Keira sat down and buried her head in the menu rather than meet the surly dark brown gaze of Patrizio's nephew across the table.

The meal was more of an ordeal than she could have ever imagined. The boys were like two snarling dogs circling each other, waiting to see who would lash out first.

It didn't help having Patrizio sitting so close to her that she could feel every contraction of his thigh muscles when he moved. Her belly quivered at the thought of how his body had felt inside her just an hour ago, her body still clamouring for the release she had not been able to achieve in that moment of madness.

She sucked in a breath when Patrizio ran his hand up her thigh beneath the table, his fingers so close to where she still pulsed and ached for him that she was sure he would be able to feel it.

'You are not eating, *cara*,' he said with a glint in his eyes. 'Or is it something else you are craving, mmm?'

'Oh, *please*,' Bruno groaned theatrically. 'You're turning me off my food.'

Patrizio eyeballed his nephew. 'You are nearly eighteen years old, Bruno. You are surely adult enough to understand how intimate relationships work. Keira and I have been separated for two months. It is to be expected that we will want to spend every moment together we can.'

'Well, don't let us keep you,' Jamie said affably. 'Unlike some people, I think it's great you've finally sorted things out. Keira has been miserable the whole time you've been apart, haven't you, Keira?'

'Yes…yes, I have,' Keira answered. 'Absolutely miserable.'

'Serves her right,' Bruno put in with another look of contempt.

Keira decided to stand up for herself and fixed him with a level stare. 'I hope that you get through life, Bruno, without making any mistakes you will later regret, but the reality is you probably won't. I made a stupid error of judgement and I've been paying for it ever since. I know it's hard for you to understand and in a way I can't help admiring you for being so loyal to your uncle, but I truly am sorry. I…I love your uncle…I have never stopped loving him.'

'Funny way of showing it, having it off with some other guy,' Bruno muttered darkly.

Patrizio leaned forward but Keira put a restraining hand on his arm. 'No, darling,' she said. 'Let me deal with this. I am to blame for what happened and I need to take responsibility for it.'

'I do not want to see you upset,' Patrizio said. 'You have not been well lately. You have suffered enough.'

Oh, how I wish you really meant those tender words, Keira thought in anguish as his fingers curled around hers.

She turned back to Bruno, her hand still enclosed in the strength and warmth of Patrizio's. 'Bruno, I'm not expecting you to forgive me for what I did, but I am asking you to please keep Jamie out of it. Any animosity you feel should be directed towards me, not him.'

'He thinks you're innocent,' Bruno said with a disdainful glance in Jamie's direction.

'She *is* innocent,' Jamie said. 'If she says she can't remember what happened that's because nothing happened. It's her word against Garth Merrick's—for all you know, he could be lying.'

If only I were innocent, Keira thought. 'Well, I'm not innocent,' she said on the tail-end of a sigh. 'I acted impulsively and wrecked several lives in the process.'

Patrizio gave her hand a gentle squeeze. 'You are forgiven, *cara*, I have told you this many times,' he said. 'Let us not waste time on rehashing the past when we have our whole future to look forward to.'

Bruno rolled his eyes. 'I still think it's all an act to get us through the last weeks of school. I bet in six weeks' time you'll be at each other's throats again.'

'In six weeks' time Keira and I will be going on a second honeymoon,' Patrizio said.

Keira only just managed to control her shock in time. She stretched her mouth into a blissful smile. 'That's right,' she said. 'I can't leave until my exhibition opens but after that we're going away together.'

'Where are you going?' Jamie asked.

'Um…'

'Paris,' Patrizio said. 'It is Keira's favourite city, isn't it, *cara*?'

'Yes,' she said, returning his smile even though it made her jaw ache. 'We had such a wonderful week there when we were first married.'

Jamie glanced at his watch and diplomatically cleared his throat. 'I hate to break things up here, but we'd better get cracking,' he said. 'I have a couple of mock exam papers to read through before lights out.'

Keira inwardly sighed as Patrizio signalled for the bill. Their act in front of the boys was coming to an end but that didn't mean the night was over.

Not by a long shot.

CHAPTER TEN

'How do you think that went?' Patrizio asked as they were driving back to South Yarra after returning the boys to the boarding house.

Keira sank her teeth into her bottom lip. 'I think Jamie believes it because he wants to,' she said. 'But your nephew is another story entirely.'

'Yes, I agree,' he said, frowning slightly as he braked at the traffic lights. 'I am not sure how to convince him.'

'Yeah, well, the second honeymoon in Paris was a stroke of genius,' she said with a hint of sarcasm. 'I certainly hope you didn't mean it.'

There was a pulsing silence, broken only by the sound of his fingers drumming on the steering wheel.

Keira swung her gaze to look at him. 'You didn't mean it…*did you*?'

His dark eyes met hers. 'I have been thinking about the time frame on our reconciliation.'

Keira felt her heart give a little jerky jump in her chest. 'You're not thinking of extending it, are you?'

He turned back to the lights. 'No, but I am concerned about what happens after the exams.'

She moistened her suddenly dry lips. 'What do you mean?'

His gaze was fixed on the road ahead. 'There will be speech night and the leavers' dinner, big events that will be rather spoilt for the boys if we go ahead with our divorce as planned.'

'So…so what are you suggesting?'

'I am suggesting that we might have to be a little flexible on the length of our reconciliation,' he said. 'It will not hurt, a week or two either way.'

She gaped at him in alarm. 'What do you mean, it wouldn't *hurt*?' she asked incredulously. 'It would hurt a lot!'

'As usual, you are making a drama out of something that is really quite simple, Keira.'

'It might appear simple to you, but it certainly doesn't to me,' she said. 'I hated every minute of acting out a lie in front of the boys. In fact I even hated acting in front of Marietta over the past couple of days. I can't help thinking she suspects something. I can't imagine maintaining this pretence for the next six days, let alone six weeks.'

'You will have to do it if I say so,' he said with an intractable edge to his tone.

Keira stiffened in her seat. 'Are you threatening me?'

'I am merely telling you that our mock reconciliation will be run by my rules and my rules only,' he said.

'You can stick your stupid rules,' she clipped out. 'I am not going to be bossed around by you.'

'You will have to do what I say this time around, Keira, otherwise you will find yourself in an untenable situation.'

She tossed her head, sending her wild curls bouncing. 'I'm not even going to ask what you mean by that,' she said. 'I really couldn't care less.'

'That is because you are still intent on being a petulant child instead of a fully grown adult,' he said. 'I had no idea when I married you how immature you really are.'

Keira felt stung by his criticism, even though she knew there was a lot of truth in what he had said. Their whirlwind courtship and marriage had not given her enough time to get to know and understand the stresses Patrizio had to deal with in terms of his life as a high profile businessman. She had resented almost from the start the way his work cut into her time with him, arguing with him and taking it far too personally when he was late or had to cancel a dinner date at the last minute. He had been patient with her at first, obviously trying to see things from her point of view, but in those last couple of weeks before the night of her leaving him she had felt his patience wearing thin. They had argued more than usual over silly little inconsequential things and many a time Keira had stormed out, threatening never to come back, never realising at the time that she would eventually do just that with such heart-wrenchingly devastating consequences.

The car purred into the driveway of his mansion and Patrizio killed the engine and swivelled in his seat to look at her. 'I think you should know that your parents came to me some months ago while we were still together. They were having trouble meeting their financial commitments.'

Keira felt a shiver scuttle up her spine like a suddenly startled mouse. 'So…' she moistened her lips '…what has that got to do with me?'

'It has everything to do with you,' he said and, stretching out an interminable pause, added, 'I have been paying your brother's private school fees ever since.'

Keira swallowed back her rising panic. 'You wouldn't go as low as to involve Jamie in this…would you?'

He gave her a cool impersonal smile. 'Not only have I been paying the rather extortionate boarding school fees of your brother, I have also paid out in full the loan your father took out to cover your university fees.'

'No…*No!*' she gasped.

He gave her one of his inscrutable looks. 'What do you think?' he asked. 'We have rather a score settle to, do we not? If I cannot get you to cooperate by other means, what choice do I have but to use coercion?'

'It's not coercion, it's blackmail.'

'Whatever.'

She gritted her teeth. 'I can't believe you would use Jamie to get at me.'

'I have already offered to pay his university and halls of residence fees for whatever course he chooses to study,' he said, as if she hadn't spoken. 'Your parents are, of course, very grateful.'

'You sick bastard,' she sniped at him. 'How else have you ingratiated yourself into my family?'

'You have always been at war with your parents but over the last couple of months I have come to realise that it probably has more to do with you than them. They have tried hard to bring you up in a decent and loving environment but you constantly kick back against their every attempt to get close to you.'

Keira felt as if he'd punched her in the middle of her stomach. In the past he had always demonstrated his understanding of how alienated she felt from her strait-laced parents. He had consoled her on so many tearful occasions when she had ranted and raved about the way her father could never give her a compliment without some pithy comment attached. Her mother had been no better, constantly criticising her for everything, including her choice of career. It hurt to think Patrizio had joined their camp when for that precious time while they had been together he had been her greatest ally.

'If I say our reconciliation will continue for as long as the boys need it to in order to make their last weeks of school as enjoyable and pleasant as possible, then it will do so,' he said into the silence, which was throbbing with tension. 'As far as I see it, you do not have any other choice.'

She sent him a caustic look. 'Have you informed your mistress that you won't be available for another couple of weeks or do you plan to sleep with her as well as with me?'

He held her defiant glare. 'This evening was an aberration,' he said. 'It is not unreasonable for ex-lovers to feel some residual attraction for each other. I think that now that we have dealt with it, it will go away.'

'You used me like a whore.'

His top lip tilted insolently. 'If that is how you behave, what else do you expect?'

She flung herself out of the car, slamming the door as hard as she could and stomping towards the house with short angry strides. 'I am not going to put up with this,' she said. 'So I slept with another man? So what? That doesn't make me a tramp.'

He caught her by the arm and turned her to face him. 'You are exactly as my nephew described you,' he bit out. 'A filthy little slut who—'

Keira only realised she had slapped his face when she heard the sound of her palm connecting with his cheek. She stood in heart-thumping shock as the red imprint of her hand gradually spread across his lean jaw.

His fingers bit into her upper arms, his eyes blazing with a hatred so intense she felt scared that he might return the action and slap her back. She shrank away from him, wincing as she physically prepared herself, her eyes closing as she waited for it to happen.

Patrizio dropped his hold as if she had burned him, his voice coming out as a scratchy rasp. 'You surely do not think I would retaliate in such a way, Keira?'

She couldn't speak, choking sobs were filling her throat and she bent her head, hugging her arms across her chest.

He let out a vicious curse and gathered her to him, his arms encircling her. 'I cannot believe you have such an appalling opinion of me,' he said in a voice she could hardly recognise as his. 'What sort of man do you think I am?'

She blubbered into his shirt front. 'I wouldn't blame you if you did. I hate myself.'

He gave her a little shake and, holding her from him, looked down at her. 'Stop this nonsense right now, Keira. I would never lay a finger on you. You are safe with me. You do realise that, don't you?'

Not safe enough, Keira thought as she looked into that dark fathomless gaze. Her bottom lip quivered uncontrollably as he held her, his body so close she could feel the warmth of it seeping into the cold loneliness of hers. 'Yes…I do know that…'

'You are overwrought and tired,' he said, leading her towards the house. 'I should have realised this evening would test your limits. Your brother knows you very well. It must have been hard to maintain the charade in front of him.'

She brushed at her eyes with the back of her hand and sniffed. 'I hated lying to him like that,' she said. 'I feel so…so…tainted…'

Patrizio frowned as he reached past her to open the door. 'I feel bad about lying to my nephew too, but what else can we do?' he asked. 'The headmaster is threatening to expel them both. We have to do whatever we can to get them through this final stage of school. If they fail their exams it will influence their career choices. Doors that close now will almost certainly close permanently.'

'I know,' she said, giving another little sniff.

He closed the door once they were inside and handed her his handkerchief. 'Here,' he said with a wry smile. 'This might be better than your sleeve.'

Keira pressed her face into the lemon-scented folds of his handkerchief. 'You must think me a total emotional wreck,' she said once she'd dealt with her streaming eyes and nose. 'Lately I seem to do nothing but cry.'

'I think you are a bit like me. We are thrown a little off course by being forced to confront our past. It is an unusual situation, no?'

'Yes,' she said, releasing an unsteady breath. 'Yes, it is…'

Patrizio carved a rough pathway through his hair with one of his hands. 'I am ashamed of how Bruno spoke to you this evening. I know a lot of young men have one rule for themselves and another for the women in their lives, but I had no idea he had such double standards.'

'Yes, well, I can see where he got his role model from,' she responded before she could stop herself. 'You have had numerous one-night stands but I have only had the one and it was with a close friend.'

'You think that somehow makes it better, do you?' he asked, his brows snapping together in anger. 'That you opened your legs for a friend rather than a total stranger?'

She held his glittering gaze with an equanimity she was nowhere close to feeling. 'So what if I did? It was one mistake. It probably only lasted three or four minutes, if that.'

'So you are starting to remember that night, are you?' he asked with a disdainful tilt to his mouth.

She had to drop her gaze from the accusing inferno of his. 'No…I just think it's a little unfair to judge me by different standards.'

'*I* did not betray our marriage vows,' he reminded her coldly. 'That was you.'

Frustration and guilt made her voice rise to a shriek as she lifted her eyes to his once more. 'I didn't do it on purpose!'

His dark gaze stripped her of what little dignity she had

left. 'Yes, you did,' he said with contempt burning in his eyes as they held hers. 'You could have chosen no better way to destroy my love and respect for you than by giving yourself to another man whilst legally married to me.'

Keira blinked back bitter tears. 'You're never going to forgive me, are you?' she asked brokenly. 'I could wear a hair shirt for the next fifty years but still you would not be able to overlook that one fall from grace.'

His eyes mercilessly raked her from head to foot. 'You will fall again, I am sure of it,' he ground out contemptuously. 'You did earlier this evening, begging for it with your body on fire for the release it craves.'

'Which you didn't deliver.' Keira knew she shouldn't have said it and certainly not in that taunting tone, but it was too late.

His dark-as-night eyes glittered with steely purpose as he pulled her towards him. 'That can easily be remedied,' he said and sent his mouth crashing down on hers.

CHAPTER ELEVEN

IF KEIRA had had more time to prepare herself for the heat and fire of his mouth she would never have responded so passionately, or so she thought in self-recrimination later. Her mouth burst into hot tongues of flame as soon as his came into contact with hers, her whole body starting to pulse with the desire that had been lurking just underneath the surface of her tingling skin for hours.

She felt the full force of his arousal against her as he held her tight in his arms, his tongue delving deeply to conquer hers. She whimpered with the sheer delight of having him so out of control, so intent on having her again in spite of how he felt about her.

He kissed with such passion, each determined thrust of his tongue reminding her of the hot hard surge of his body in hers. Her body prepared itself; the silky scented dew of arousal made her legs soften with surrender as he manoeuvred her towards the sumptuous lounge.

He pressed her down to the carpet at their feet, his hands beginning to remove her clothes, each stroke or glide of fabric along her skin a sensuous caress under-girded with urgency.

She gasped out loud when his mouth closed over one tight nipple, his tongue rolling and curling until she was writhing with pleasure beneath the weight of his body. Her legs tangled with his, her hips lifting off the carpeted floor to feel more of his potency where she so desperately needed it.

Patrizio might not love her any more but this was one way she could show how much she loved him, Keira thought as she caressed his back and shoulders with her hands, her body aching to be possessed by his.

He lifted his head from her breast and met her passion-glazed eyes. 'Tell me you want me, Keira,' he commanded as he began stroking her intimately.

'I want you…'

'Louder.'

'I want you.'

His eyes glittered with triumph. 'Say my name. Say it, Keira, say who it is you want.'

She was almost sobbing with desperation as his fingers moved rhythmically against her swollen point of need. 'I want you, Patrizio…Oh, God, I want you so much…'

She shuddered as her orgasm rolled through her in wave after wave of release, each nerve and sinew in her body trembling with the aftershocks. She was boneless, a melted pool of femininity in his arms.

She opened her eyes to meet his, the dark unreadable depths of his gaze making her belly quiver with uncertainty.

'Who were you thinking of when you came?' he asked.

She frowned at him. 'W-what sort of question is that?'

He cupped her right breast in his hand, his eyes like a laser beam on hers. 'I want you to think of me and only me this time,' he said. 'Do you understand? Me. Not your childhood sweetheart, but me.'

Keira gave a choked gasp as he moved down her body, his mouth leaving hot moist kisses all over her flesh, from breast to trembling thigh. She knew what was coming and her whole body shivered in anticipation. The first intimate glide of his tongue against her lifted her back off the floor; the second had her clinging to him with claw-like fingers, her breathing becoming rapid and uneven as he subjected her to the most erotic assault on her senses possible. She gasped, she panted, she screamed with the sheer force of it, her entire body feeling as if an earthquake had passed through it.

She had barely come back down to earth before he was thrusting deep inside her, hard, hot and heavy, his low-pitched grunts of pleasure as he set a frantic rhythm making her body tingle all over again. She clung to him as he rocked against her, her senses spinning out of control all over again as he brought her closer and closer to the edge of reason.

His mouth coming down on hers smothered her moaning cries of ecstasy. She felt his body bucking with the force of his own release, the soft pads of her fingers feeling the lift of his flesh as he gave a whole-body shiver of reaction.

His breathing was still choppy as he propped himself up on his elbows to look down at her. 'Did Merrick ever make you come three times in a row?' he asked.

Keira closed her eyes, the twin blades of pain and shame slicing at her insides. 'Stop it, Patrizio…please.'

'Look at me.'

She scrunched her eyes tighter. 'No.'

'Look at me, damn it!' he growled as he grasped her by the upper arms.

She looked at him with tears shining in her eyes. 'Why are you spoiling the special thing we just shared?' she choked. 'You're making it feel so tawdry and cheap.'

He lifted himself off her in one fluid movement, tucking in his shirt and re-zipping himself as he looked down at her with flinty disdain. 'That is because what we just shared is tawdry and cheap,' he said. 'It was just sex. Good sex, I am prepared to admit, but, as for being special—no.'

Keira felt his words like a stake going through her heart. How could he be so cruel? Even though shame coursed through her as she fumbled her way back into her clothes, she wasn't going to give him the satisfaction of grinding her pride to powder beneath the heel of his shoe. She had made love with him because she loved him. He could cheapen it all he liked but she would always treasure every moment she spent in his arms.

But then she wasn't the only person who had been in his arms lately, she reminded herself painfully. Somehow she couldn't see him describing his intimate moments with the elegant Gisela Hunter in such crude terms.

'I probably should have asked you this earlier, but I am assuming you are still on the pill?' he said into the simmering silence.

Keira felt her fingers momentarily stall on the fastening of her bra and hoped he hadn't noticed. She adjusted her clothing and lifted her chin to meet his steady gaze. 'I happened to notice you've dropped your safe sex standards,' she said with a cutting edge to her voice. 'I hope I'm not going to get some nasty little infection passed on from one of your many girlfriends.'

His mouth tightened. 'If anyone should be concerned about being infected, it should be me,' he returned coolly.

She gave him a caustic glare. 'You're such a bastard.'

'You did not answer my question,' he reminded her. 'Are you currently using a reliable method of contraception?'

She rolled her lips together, trying to avoid his gaze. She had stopped taking the low dose pill weeks ago. She didn't even know where the packet was now.

'Keira?'

'Um...yes.' She stumbled through her reply. 'I'm covered.'

His dark gaze held hers. 'If there is any doubt in your

mind, you need to tell me now,' he said. 'If you were to conceive a child, it would be very hard to…' He paused, as if wondering whether to continue.

'Go on, say it,' she put in bitterly. 'Don't spare my feelings, Patrizio.'

'I am not sure what you are referring to. I was merely going to say—'

'I know what you were going to say,' she said through tight lips, her eyes flashing with resentment. 'You were going to say it would be hard to prove paternity, weren't you?'

'As far as I am aware, a simple test can give us that information if we need to do so,' he said. 'But no, I was not going to say that at all."

Keira felt herself backing down. 'Oh…well, then…sorry…I thought…'

'I was going to say it would be hard to justify going through with a divorce if we conceive a child,' he said. 'Don't you agree?'

She looked at him in wide-eyed surprise. 'Are you mad?'

'Not mad, just thinking of the child caught in the middle,' he said.

'A baby is not part of a marriage repair kit,' she said. 'If anything, a child would put even more stress on a relationship that's going nowhere. Besides, imagine the emotional damage to a child growing up with parents who despise each other. That is tantamount to abuse.'

'What would you do if it happened?'

'You mean if I got pregnant?'

He nodded.

She swallowed as she tried to remember when she had last had a period and her heart began to hammer with panic as she did the sums.

Surely it hadn't been *that* long?

She had been sick with the flu, which had disrupted her cycle.

That was it, surely. Besides, coming off the pill could make things go a little haywire, she reasoned. There was no way she could have…

She shrank back from where her thoughts were heading. 'It's not going to happen, Patrizio,' she said, wondering if it already had. The only trouble was, how on earth was she going to tell him? Panic rushed through her until her head began to spin with it. She hadn't had a period for two months, which meant… She gulped in shock. *Oh, God, how would she even know for sure whose child it was?*

Patrizio frowned at her subdued tone and slumped posture. Her face was milk-white, the tiny dusting of freckles sprinkled over her nose standing out in stark relief from the pallor of her skin.

His chest felt tighter than it should, as if his heart had swollen to twice its size. He was finding it harder and harder to maintain his anger towards her. He had even begun to wonder if what Jamie had hinted at was true. Perhaps Keira didn't remember anything because nothing had actually happened—it was, after all, Merrick's word against hers. Patrizio wasn't sure of the motivation behind such an action, although he suspected jealousy would be way up there somewhere. Merrick had been a constant presence in Keira's social life until he had come on the scene and swept her off her feet.

He took a step towards her, his hand going to the satin-softness of her arm, his fingers curling around her wrist like a bracelet. 'Is there any chance—any chance at all—that Merrick lied to you about what happened that night?' he asked, wondering for the first time why he hadn't asked her this before.

Keira blinked back tears as she lifted her gaze to his. 'I don't know… Why would he do that?'

His thumb stroked back and forth over her thudding pulse. 'We married within a matter of weeks of meeting. He might have felt cast aside or something. It can happen in close relationships—one party resents the new-found happiness of the other.'

She gnawed at her lips as she thought of those rumpled sheets and her naked body lying amongst them.

'Cara?' he prompted.

'No…' Her voice was not even audible.

'I can't hear you, Keira.'

She compressed her lips even tighter as the tears filled her eyes as she met his gaze. 'I'm sorry…but I don't think he was lying.'

His hand fell away from her wrist. 'So we are back to square one,' he said heavily.

'Only if you choose not to forgive me,' she said in a small voice.

He scraped a hand through his hair as he put some distance between them. 'I wish I could, but it is just too close to home,' he said, leaning one hand against the wall, his head hanging down as if in defeat.

Keira frowned at the hollowness of his tone. 'What do you mean?'

He turned and straightened with a grim look. 'Do you remember I told you my father was injured in a car accident several years before he died?'

'Yes, of course I remember. It was so sad. I don't know how he coped with being permanently disabled. It must have been truly devastating.'

'Yes, well, he coped with it a whole lot better than my mother.'

Keira unconsciously held her breath. Patrizio had rarely spoken of his parents; he seemed to avoid the subject whenever she had raised it but she had assumed it was because he felt so helpless over his father's disability and his death from cancer a few years later.

'My mother had several affairs with other men after my father's accident,' he said. 'She didn't bother hiding it. I think in a way she was proud of it. It disgusted me to see her cavorting with whoever was available while my father sat strapped in his chair, unable to even feed himself.'

Keira felt her heart tighten at the thought of how his father must have suffered. It made Patrizio's anger towards her all the more understandable. He must have felt as betrayed as his father had done and, with the frenzied activity of the press violating his privacy over the last two months, just as helpless.

'I wish you had told me all this before,' she said.

'What difference would it have made?' he asked. 'Would it have stopped you behaving the way you did?'

Keira had no answer. Guilt and regret were her constant companions and had been ever since that night. What she had done was beyond belief. She had never thought herself capable of such wanton behaviour.

'Go to bed, Keira,' he said after a short but tense silence. 'You have shadows upon shadows under your eyes. You look like you haven't slept properly for weeks.'

Eight weeks, she thought as he moved towards the door, but she didn't say it out loud. What would be the point? He didn't want to hear how she had cried her heart out for the mistake she had made. He wanted her to pay for it indefinitely, by reminding her at every opportunity of what she had thrown away. That was why he was determined to divorce her. Forgiveness wasn't a word he had in his vocabulary.

'Are you coming to bed now too?' she asked instead.

He turned and raked her with his eyes. 'Not satisfied yet, Keira?'

She straightened her shoulders, what little pride she had left glittering in her gaze as she forced herself to meet his. 'I will never be satisfied until you look at me with respect instead of hatred and loathing in your eyes,' she said.

His mouth tilted sardonically. 'Then you will be waiting a very long time, *tesoro mio*.'

'Don't insult me by calling me that when you don't mean it,' she threw back angrily. 'I am not your treasure. I am more like your trash.'

His eyes roved over her mercilessly again. 'I could not have put it better myself,' he said and, with a mocking smile, moved through the door, closing it gently but firmly behind him.

CHAPTER TWELVE

KEIRA didn't think she was capable of sleep in her emotional turmoil but somehow she finally drifted off. She woke just as the sun was sending golden fingers of light through the curtains, casting a warm glow over Patrizio, lying beside her, his features calm and relaxed in sleep.

She ached to reach out and touch him as she had done so many times in the past. One fingertip tiptoeing down his body was all it would take to have him turning towards her, fully erect, his dark eyes glinting as she closed her hand around him.

She moistened her mouth as she thought of how she had tasted him, the salty musk of his skin filling her senses, rocking her to the core of her being when he'd responded so passionately in the past.

She opened and closed her fingers lying so close to his thigh. It was so tempting, so very tempting, to reach out and touch him, to feel the surge of his blood as he reacted to her intimate caress…

Keira blinked in shock when he suddenly captured her hand and brought it to his groin, his eyes still closed, his sleepy groan of pleasure as her fingers instinctively explored him making her stomach tilt sideways.

'Yes, *cara*,' he said in a gravelly tone. 'That is just the way I like it.'

Her throat went dry as she felt him leap under her touch, his thickening flesh already hard against the softness of her hand. Acting on an impulse she couldn't control even if she had wanted to, she moved down his body with her mouth pressing soft-as-air kisses on to each of his dark pebbly nipples, down the length of his sternum, poking her tongue into the hairy indentation of his belly button before going lower. She felt him suck in his breath, his abdomen taut with anticipation as her tongue slid along his shaft, rolling over the most sensitive point in tantalising little cat-like licks until she finally closed her mouth over him. She felt him buck in response, his rasping groan coming from deep within him as she took him to paradise and swallowed the evidence.

He gave a languorous stretch before he captured her gaze with his. 'I am starting to think that six months' instead of six weeks' reconciliation would be very tempting,' he said with a taunting smile. 'What do you say, Keira? Do you want to have a little affair with me before we get a divorce?'

Keira knew she had betrayed herself by worshipping his body the way she had. It upset her that within seconds of her caresses he was mentioning their divorce, as if to remind her of her precarious place in his life. Any involvement they had would have legal papers signed at the end of it and she had better not forget it.

She gave him a withering look. 'You have *got* to be joking.'

He placed his hand on the silky skin of her shoulder to stop her rolling away. 'Think about it, *cara*,' he said. 'We are so good together, you know we are. You make me crazy with desire, just looking at me the way you are doing right now.'

'I'm not looking at you…like that…'

'Yes, you are,' he said, forcing her chin up. 'You look at me so hungrily, as if you could never get enough of me.'

'You're imagining it.'

He brushed the tip of his tongue across the tight seam of her lips, raising his head to lock gazes with her again. 'You think I am imagining the tremble of your body?' he asked, cupping her breast.

'I—I'm not trembling…'

'Do you think I am imagining the way you keep running your tongue over your lips in anticipation of my kiss?'

'I don't do that,' she said, having just done it.

He smiled and moved his weight over her, trapping her beneath him. 'Am I imagining the silk of your inner thighs, *cara*? The way you open them for me so I can do this?'

Oh, God, Keira thought as his long fingers entered her. She had no hope of denying what she felt for him when he did that. She melted, her whole body sinking into the mattress as he replaced his fingers with his thickened length, the first deep thrust filling her completely, making her cry out in pleasure.

'Am I imagining you writhing beneath me as you are now, Keira?' he asked as he increased his pace.

'No…' she gasped as he stroked her to enhance her pleasure. 'No…no…'

'So it is true, is it not? That you want me desperately, all the time, in any place, in any position, right, Keira?'

'Yes…oh, yes…'

She tensed as he held her over the precipice, dangling her there until she began to beg. 'Please…oh, please…*now!*'

He pushed her over with another deep thrust, the rolling waves of release tossing her about like a rag doll until she was totally limp in his arms. She felt his shuddering explosion inside her, the muscles on his back taut as a bow as he emptied himself, the scent of sexual intimacy filling her nostrils.

The silence settled in the room like dust motes after a hot breeze had blown through an opened door.

Keira could hear the sound of her heart beating, the roar of her blood making her feel light-headed. Again she felt as if she had betrayed herself to him. It would no doubt please him to know she still had feelings for him; it would make his victory complete to cast her from him when they finally divorced.

An aching sadness filled her as if it were being drip-fed into her bloodstream, making her body feel heavy and lethargic with grief at how her life had turned out. Patrizio was within touching distance, she still had the essence of him in her most feminine place, and yet he was a world away from her in terms of bitterness and hate.

The mattress shifted beneath his weight as he got up. 'I have to get to work,' he said. 'Do you need a lift to college?'

She pulled the sheets up over her nakedness. 'No,' she said, avoiding his eyes. 'I can make my own way by tram.'

'What happened to your car?' he asked.

'I had to sell it.'

Patrizio frowned. 'Why?'

She gave a little shrug of one shoulder. 'I needed the money for paint and canvases.'

'I can organise a car for you,' he said after a short pause. 'Would you like me to do that?'

She shook her head, still not looking at him. He moved back towards the bed and, leaning down, hitched up her chin so she had to look into his eyes. 'I will make sure a car is delivered to you as soon as possible,' he said. 'You can have it as long as you want.'

'I don't want you to do that, Patrizio,' she said. 'It doesn't seem right.'

He straightened from the bed. 'Consider it payment for

services rendered,' he said with an up and down sweep of his gaze over her body.

Her violet-blue eyes glittered with sparks of anger. 'That's disgusting.'

He lifted one brow. 'But accurate, no?'

'No,' she said, tightening her hands into fists. 'I didn't sleep with you for any other reason than…than…'

'Than what, Keira?' he asked. 'Old times' sake?'

She ran her tongue over her lips, the slight tremble of her chin making Patrizio wonder if she had been as affected by him as he was by her. His body still tingled where she had touched him, the scent of her skin was on his and the sweet taste of her lips was indelibly imprinted on his.

A short-term affair should just about do it, he thought. It would get her out of his system once and for all. He would leave when he felt it was time to quit. He would dictate the terms this time around; he wouldn't leave himself vulnerable to her betrayal again.

'Why did you sleep with me, Keira?' he asked into the ticking silence.

'You know why,' she said so softly that he almost didn't hear it.

'Because you just could not help yourself, right?' he said with a derisive twist to his mouth. 'Because you are a highly sensual woman who is always on the lookout for a playmate, right?'

'No, that's not what I meant at all.'

He made a move towards the *en suite* bathroom. 'I am happy to keep you occupied for the next six weeks, a couple of months even if you are agreeable, but after that we are getting divorced as planned.'

'I'm not sleeping with you again,' she said with a determined jut of her chin. 'We were supposed to be pretending to be reconciled, remember?'

He gave her a cool little smile. 'We are pretending, yes, but why not have our cake and eat it too?'

She folded her arms across her breasts. 'This cake is not for sale.'

'Every cake is for sale, Keira,' he said, raking her with his gaze. 'Even yours.'

Keira responded by throwing the sheets over her head, but the sound of his mocking laugh as he went into the *en suite* bathroom taunted her long after he had left for the office.

'How are you going with your exhibition?' Harriet Fuller, one of the other Masters students, asked at college later that day.

'I'm not quite finished,' Keira confessed, brushing a curl away from her face as she looked up from the painting she was working on.

Harriet peered over her shoulder. 'Not bad,' she said. 'You like your strong colours, don't you?'

'You think it's too much?'

Harriet tapped her lips. 'No, not really. It's distinctive, eye-catching, if you like.'

Keira chewed on the end of the brush for a moment before confessing, 'I just hope someone likes it enough to buy it or one of the others.'

'Yeah, well, that's the dream, isn't it?' Harriet said with a wistful smile. 'All of us here want to make a living from our art but it's hardly likely to happen. We have to die first to become famous.'

Keira sighed as she put her brush down. 'Yes, I guess you're right.'

'I saw that thing in the paper the other day,' Harriet said. 'Is it true? Are you back with your husband, Patrizio?'

'Yes…yes, it's true,' Keira answered and, shifting her gaze back to her painting, added, 'it's early days yet, though…'

'So this is sort of a trial reconciliation?' Harriet asked.

'We're just taking it one day at a time.'

'I bet your parents are pleased,' Harriet said.

'Yeah…they are…'

'Are you OK, Keira?' Harriet asked with a frown. 'You seem a bit spaced out.'

'I'm fine, just tired. It's a busy time of year.'

'I guess that gorgeous husband of yours is keeping you up all hours, huh?'

Keira tried to smile but it made her face feel strange. 'Something like that…'

'I'd better get moving,' Harriet said. 'Good luck with the portfolio.'

'Thanks.'

'And good luck with your marriage. He's a good man, Keira. Believe me, they're pretty hard to come by these days.'

Keira picked up her brush again and inwardly sighed. Patrizio had been the nicest man she'd ever met until the day he'd found her in bed with Garth. After that he had turned into someone else entirely.

A stranger.

An angry and bitter stranger who wanted her to have an affair with him before they eventually divorced.

Could she do it?

Could she risk what little self-respect she'd mustered over the last two months in the fragile hope of making him fall in love with her all over again? He was still fiercely attracted to her, which was some sort of compensation to her shattered pride, she supposed. But he only wanted her to share his bed, nothing else. It was hard not to feel a little short-changed. She knew it was a lot to ask for a man, and a proud Italian one at that, to overlook a misdemeanour such as hers. She even wondered if she would be able to do it herself if the boot had been on the other foot as she had initially suspected. The thought of him sharing his body with other women had tortured her from day one of their marriage. Her inbuilt insecurity had nibbled away at her, making her react in an entirely immature and foolish way, when instead she should have confronted him with the issue in a calm and rational manner.

What clear vision one had via the retrospect-scope, Keira thought wryly. But what would turning back the clock achieve when she didn't even remember what had happened that night?

The memory was locked somewhere deep in her brain—perhaps *she* had locked it out to escape responsibility for her actions. Suppression of memories was a tricky subject; there were convincing arguments on both sides. What if she had shut down that memory because it was too painful to confront the truth of her infidelity?

But then another thought slipped into her head. She tried to quickly push it aside, not wanting to think for a moment that Garth would wilfully destroy her reputation and marriage, but still the thought lingered like a fog, clouding her brain until she wasn't sure what to think any more. Yes, she had confided in Garth many times in the early months of her marriage, speaking of her doubts of Patrizio remaining faithful when he was away such a lot but Garth had always been supportive and reassuring. She had no reason to believe that he would betray her when for so long he had been her closest friend.

But Garth was no longer her closest confidante, she reminded herself with a deep pang of regret. He was virtually a stranger now; she hadn't seen or heard from him in weeks.

But if what she suspected was true, he would have to be told, Keira thought with another wave of sickening panic. He had the right to know that he was one of two possible candidates if it turned out she was indeed pregnant.

The testing kit was still in her handbag; she hadn't yet summoned up the courage to use it. She knew she was doing her usual procrastination routine but every time she put her hand in her bag for something she felt as if she were physically touching her guilt and shame.

The thought of telling Patrizio was something she couldn't even think about. He hadn't been able to forgive her for sleeping with another man—how on earth would he forgive her for falling pregnant as a result of that one night of infidelity? How could he ever love her again, knowing she was carrying another man's child?

He would never take her back permanently.

She couldn't ask it of him.

She placed a hand on her stomach, her heart squeezing painfully. She had longed for a child with Patrizio; how cruel would it be if it turned out not to be his? She knew she would love it regardless—it was totally innocent in the wreckage she had made of her life—but it would haunt her for the rest of her days that her impetuous actions had led to yet another life being a casualty.

She reached past the testing kit in her bag for her phone and looked at it for a full thirty seconds, her forehead furrowed with indecision. Then, drawing in a breath that caught at her throat like a twig being swallowed, she slowly began dialling…

CHAPTER THIRTEEN

'GARTH?' Keira held the mobile closer to her ear to block out the noise of the students passing the studio. 'It's me—Keira.'

'Oh…Hi, Keira,' Garth said. 'Um…I was going to call you. I wanted you to be the first to know my news.'

'What news is that?' she asked.

'I'm moving to Canada. I'm getting married. I'm leaving in just over a month.'

'Congratulations. Mum mentioned something about you seeing someone from abroad. I'm really happy for you.'

'Yeah, well, thanks,' he said and, clearing his throat, added, 'I hear you got back with Patrizio.'

'Yes,' she said perhaps a little too brightly. 'I'm very happy.'

'That's great, then…great.'

'Garth, I was wondering if we could meet up some time to chat,' she said. 'Are you free in the next day or so?'

'I'm pretty busy, what with planning the wedding and all…'

'It's really important,' she said. 'It's about…about that night.'

'Look, Keira, it's best if we just forget about it. It happened, OK? I don't want my fiancée to hear about it. I've put it behind me and so should you.'

'I think I'm pregnant.'

'That's wonderful, Keira,' he said. 'That's absolutely wonderful news. I'm happy for you. It's what you've always wanted.'

'Garth...you don't understand...' She gulped in a ragged breath. 'It could be yours...'

There was a long pulsating silence.

'Garth, did you hear me?' she asked.

'Yes...' he said, his voice sounding like a stranger's. 'Yes, I heard you.'

'I don't know what to do...I'm so scared...'

'It can't be mine, Keira.'

'How can you be so sure?' she asked.

'How many weeks are you?'

'I don't know. I haven't even done a test yet. I've been putting it off. I can't bear the thought of telling Patrizio.'

'You should see a doctor and have the dates confirmed,' he said. 'I am sure you will find that rules me out.'

There was another silence.

'He hasn't forgiven me, Garth. We're not really back together. We're only doing it because of Bruno and Jamie.' She explained the situation between the two boys and added, 'It's killing me to have Patrizio back in my life with this horrible thing between us. I just need to understand how it happened.'

'I told you what happened.'

'Tell me again, bit by bit. I don't care how embarrassing it is. I just need to know what led me to—'

'I'm sorry, but I have to go. Mischa's going to be phoning me any minute.'

'Garth, please I—'

'Stop it, Keira,' he said, cutting her off again. 'There's no point in pursuing this. I have to go. Goodbye.'

Keira stared at the mobile, the dial tone sounding deafening in the accusing silence...

* * *

The house was quiet when she got home, which somehow made Keira feel even more desperately alone. Every room seemed to contain a hint of Patrizio's aftershave, which made her heart contract to the point of pain when she thought of the final curtain coming down on their marriage. How would she survive it? How would she cope without seeing him every day? The last two months had shattered her both emotionally and physically; God only knew what would happen to her if he cut her from his life for good.

She went upstairs to the bedroom and, taking the pregnancy test kit out of her bag, looked at it for a long moment. She was torn between wanting to know for sure and wanting to pretend it wasn't happening. It was cowardly of her, she knew, but she stuffed it in her underwear drawer, covering it haphazardly with piles of lace.

She let out a shaky breath and walked back to the bed, where she had dumped her bag, and took out her mobile. 'Mum? Have you got a minute to talk?' she asked once her mother had answered.

'Oh, I'm glad you called, Keira,' Robyn said in a bustling tone. 'I tried to call you earlier but you were engaged. I've spoken to Patrizio and he's accepted our invitation to dinner this evening.'

'Well, it wouldn't be the first time, I imagine,' Keira said with a touch of pique.

'I hope you're not going to be petulant about our ongoing relationship with him.' Her mother sighed. 'He's taken you back and you should be very grateful, although how long for is anyone's guess.'

Keira felt her heart kick against her sternum. 'What do you mean by that?' she asked.

'You know what you're like, Keira, getting your knickers

in a twist over nothing. I'm terrified you're going to ruin things again with your willful, erratic behaviour.'

'Thanks for the vote of confidence, Mum, it's exactly what every insecure girl needs from her mother.'

'You're not insecure, you're immature,' Robyn said. 'You've had everything that money could buy and still you're not happy. For God's sake, what else do you want from us?'

Keira felt tears at the backs of her eyes. 'I want to be accepted for who I am,' she said. 'Is that so much to ask?'

'You are talking rubbish again, Keira,' her mother said dismissively. 'Your father and I have done all we can to support you, but you seem incapable of being grateful.'

'Do you love me, Mum?' she asked.

'What sort of question is that?'

'It's the sort of question insecure daughters need to ask occasionally.'

'Keira, I am finding this conversation very upsetting,' Robyn said. 'Of course I love you; you're my daughter.'

'Does Dad love me?'

'Keira, please, this is ridiculous—'

'Does he?'

'Of course he does.'

'He's never said it to me. Not once.'

'He's not the openly affectionate type,' Robyn said. 'You know that.'

'He's openly affectionate to Jamie.'

'Yes, well, that's probably a father and son bonding thing,' her mother said. 'Now, stop asking all these silly questions. We'll see you tonight at seven.'

'Mum?'

'Keira, I have to check on the roast.'

'Is a leg of lamb more important to you than your own daughter?'

Robyn let out a sigh. 'Are you having trouble with Patrizio?'

'No,' she lied. 'I just feel a bit emotional right now.' *And I think I'm pregnant and I don't know who the father is*, she added in wretched despair.

'Patrizio's a good man, Keira. Don't get it wrong this time around. So many men wouldn't have taken you back. There are very few marriages that survive when it's the wife that strays. You should be very grateful, very grateful indeed.'

'I am…I am grateful…'

'See you tonight; the boys are coming too. Your father is picking them up from the boarding house on the way home,' Robyn said, her tone losing its sharp edge as she added, 'I've made your favourite dessert.'

She brushed at her eyes with the back of her hand. 'Thanks, Mum,' she said and went to say, I love you, but her mother had already hung up.

Keira let out a sigh as her eyes drifted back to the walk-in wardrobe. After another moment's deliberation, she stood up and went back to the underwear drawer and took out the pregnancy testing kit and then, taking a deep breath, headed for the bathroom.

Patrizio found Keira in the lounge room, sitting on the edge of one of the sofas chewing at what was left of her nails. She dropped her hand from her mouth with a guilty flush and got to her feet. 'Mum said she called you about dinner,' she said. 'The boys are coming too.'

'Yes,' he said, running his gaze over her frail-looking form. 'But if you are not feeling up to it, we don't have to go.'

Something flickered briefly in her eyes before she lowered them to stare at the floor. 'I'm fine.'

He stepped towards her and put a hand on her shoulder, frowning when she flinched slightly. 'What's going on, Keira?'

Keira lifted her eyes to his. 'Nothing's going on. I'm just a little tired and run-down.' *And pregnant*, she tacked on in silent desperation. The test kit with its lines of truth was upstairs on her sweater shelf this time, hidden under thick layers of wool where she hoped Marietta wouldn't find it.

He held her gaze for endless moments, her heart beginning to flutter with fear that he would see for himself what she was so desperately trying to conceal. She needed more time to prepare herself mentally for his reaction to her news. She knew it was yet another example of her tendency to stall over things she found difficult to deal with, but this time she just couldn't help it. Her baby's future was at stake. She wanted to do everything possible to provide a safe and secure future for it, no matter what.

'I bought you a car,' he said into the thrumming silence. 'It's being delivered first thing in the morning.'

She tried to smile but her lips felt stiff and awkward. 'Thank you…but you didn't need to go to that sort of trouble. I'm used to using public transport.'

'I would prefer you to use the car I have bought,' he said. 'I do not want the press wondering why my wife is hopping on and off trams while I have a luxury car and driver at my disposal.'

'So it's all about appearances then, is it?' she asked with an edge of bitterness distorting her tone.

'But of course,' he said. 'That is why we are continuing with this charade, is it not?'

'It seems to me this has gone way past a charade,' she said. 'I don't know what's real and what's false any more.'

He snatched up the keys he had not long put down. 'Yes, well, that has been your problem from the start, has it not?'

She turned away in distress. 'Stop it, Patrizio. Please just stop it. I can't take any more of this. Not now.'

Patrizio felt a twinge of remorse pull at him deep inside. She was obviously exhausted and trying hard to keep on top of things. She was coming to the end of her academic year, which was stressful enough, and with the boys' issues things had probably tipped her over. 'I am sorry, Keira,' he said. 'It has been a lot to ask of you at this time but we have to try and maintain appearances for the boys' sake.'

'I know…I'm doing my best…'

He put his hands on her shoulders and took some measure of comfort that this time she didn't flinch away. 'I know you are, *cara*,' he said gently. 'You are doing a magnificent job of convincing everyone you are still in love with me.'

She slowly turned in his arms, her eyes not reaching the full distance to his. 'We should go,' she said in a husky tone. 'Mum's gone to a lot of trouble. I don't want to disappoint her by turning up late.'

They were a little late arriving at her parents' house but Jamie and Bruno had not long come in with Keira's father, so they were still in the process of receiving drinks and putting school blazers to one side.

Jamie came over to Keira once everyone was organised and smiled at her warmly. 'How cool is this? Mum and Dad haven't had me home for a meal during the week in term time for months.'

'Is boarding school so very bad?' she asked with a concerned look.

Her brother shifted his gaze. 'Not really,' he said. 'Things have been a bit rough lately but I think we're gradually sorting it out.'

Keira's gaze flicked to where Bruno was being spoken to by a heavily frowning Patrizio. 'Bruno doesn't look too happy to be here tonight,' she observed.

'Yes, well, he's in the enemy camp so to speak,' Jamie said. 'I'm sorry about the stuff he said about you the other night. I wanted to punch his lights out.'

'It will hopefully blow over now that Patrizio and I are back together.'

Jamie gave her a probing look. 'It is for real, isn't it, Kiki?' he asked, using his childhood mispronunciation of her name for the first time in years. 'I mean you're not just staging this to get us through the exams or something, are you?'

Keira had a lot of trouble holding his intently focused gaze. 'We're still feeling our way but it's very real,' she said, her mind filling with images of her lovemaking with Patrizio. 'We belong together, Jamie. It's what we both want.'

'I told Bruno it was genuine but he's not convinced,' he said.

'What would convince him?' she asked.

He shifted his lips back and forth in a musing pose. 'I'm not sure,' he said. 'Have you thought about publicly restating your vows?'

Her eyes flicked back to Patrizio, her stomach tilting when she found he was looking at her. She forced her lips into a strained help-me smile before turning back to her brother. 'We haven't discussed it but maybe you should ask Patrizio.'

'Ask me what?' Patrizio asked as he slipped an arm around Keira's waist.

Jamie faced him with an engaging smile. 'I was wondering if you were going to make a public declaration of your recommitment, you know, like a renewal of wedding vows.'

Patrizio looked down at Keira. 'What do you think, *cara*?' he asked. 'Do you fancy being my bride for the second time around?'

She moistened her lips. 'I'm not sure it's necessary to go to all that fuss for—'

'I told you it's not real,' Bruno said with a sneer as he moved across the room to join them. 'She won't do it because as soon as she gets a chance she's going to be off with her lover.'

'Bruno, I have already warned you about speaking to your aunt—'

Bruno's defiant glare cut off his uncle's reprimand. 'Why don't you check her mobile phone?' he suggested. 'Scroll through the dialled or received calls and I can almost guarantee you'll find she's still in contact with him.'

Keira felt as if every drop of blood was draining out of her limbs to pool in her cheeks. Her tongue stuck like a sweaty sock to the roof of her mouth, and her stomach rolled in panic as her worried gaze went to her purse where her mobile phone lay concealed in silence, with all the evidence to convict her at the touch of a button.

'You are wrong,' Patrizio said as he drew Keira even closer. 'I do not need to go to such devious lengths to check up on her. We have re-established trust and will now move forward, with the past in the past where it belongs.'

'Once a tart, always a tart,' Bruno said under his breath but loud enough for them to hear it.

'Dinner is ready!' Robyn said with cheery brightness. 'Come on, boys, sit yourselves down and tuck in.'

Patrizio held Keira back as the boys went to the table. 'It's not working,' he said in a harsh whisper. 'We are going to have to try harder.'

'What do you suggest we do?' she asked, looking up at him worriedly.

He glanced towards the boys, who were accepting plates laden with roast lamb and vegetables. 'I do not know but we will have to do something and do it soon,' he said and led her towards the table.

CHAPTER FOURTEEN

KEIRA took her place beside Patrizio and made an effort to do justice to the meal her mother had prepared but it was hard going. Her stomach was still churning at the thought of telling Patrizio of her pregnancy. She couldn't imagine how he would receive the news, certainly not with delight, that much was sure.

Every now and again she felt his thigh brush hers beneath the table and her nerves would start fizzing with reaction at the thought of being in his arms again, but for how long was, as her mother had hinted at earlier that day, anybody's guess.

The boys were seated opposite each other and, while Jamie was clearly doing his best to ignore the acid burn of Bruno's glare from time to time, he wasn't so lucky when it came to avoiding his father's questions as to why his grades had slipped so appallingly.

Keira hated seeing her brother's shoulders begin to slump as their father continued his red wine–fuelled tirade and eventually she could stand it no longer and confronted him when he paused to take a breath. 'Don't you think it's a little hypocritical of you to be so critical of Bruno's bullying of Jamie when you are doing it to him yourself?'

'What did you say?' Kingsley glared at her.

Keira put her chin up. 'You heard me, Dad. Stop going on at Jamie. You're always chipping away at him; no wonder he finds it hard to stand up for himself when other people have a go at him. You've been systematically destroying his self-esteem like you have done to me for as long as I can remember.'

Patrizio's hand came to hers where it was gripping the edge of the table. '*Cara.*'

She turned her angry expression his way. 'Keep out of it, Patrizio,' she said, slipping her hand out from under his. 'This is between my father and me.'

'You're talking rubbish as usual,' Kingsley said. 'The boy needs toughening up. A bit of bullying doesn't go astray now and again. I've had plenty of it in my time and it didn't hurt me.'

Keira rolled her eyes in frustration. 'That's exactly my point. You've obviously been the target of a bully in the past and now you're carrying on the pattern to the next generation.'

'Thanks for the support, Keira, but I can stand up for myself,' Jamie said as he eyeballed his father. 'I am doing what I can to get through the next few weeks. I know it will be a huge disappointment to you and Mum if I don't make the grade for medical or law school, but have you ever thought that maybe I don't want to be a doctor or a lawyer?'

Keira watched as her parents exchanged horrified glances.

'But you have to do *something* with your life!' Kingsley was the first to find his voice. 'You're not thinking of being an artist or something equally time-wasting like your sister, are you?'

'Keira is a very talented painter, Mr Worthington,' Patrizio said with dignified calm. 'You should be very proud of her achievements.'

Although Keira knew he was only maintaining the façade

of their reunion, she still felt a swell of her heart at his vote of confidence. She gave him a grateful glance and her belly did a little flip-flop as she encountered the warmth in his gaze.

'Surely it's up to me to decide what I want to do with my life,' Jamie argued.

'Not when I'm paying, it's not!' Kingsley said.

'But you're not paying, are you?' Keira put in with a challenging look. 'Patrizio has been seeing to all that, hasn't he?'

Kingsley pulled his mouth tight and rose from the table in one clumsy movement. 'He's a fool for taking you back,' he said with spittle forming at the corners of his mouth. 'I've got a good mind to tell him the truth about your—'

'No, Kingsley,' Robyn said with a desperate edge to her tone. 'Please…'

Keira felt her body stiffen as she watched her father turn from the table and leave the room. She swallowed convulsively as her mother got unsteadily to her feet, her face pinched and white as she began to clear away the plates in a mechanical fashion. 'Mum?'

Robyn Worthington pasted an overly bright smile on her face. 'Dessert, anyone?' she asked. 'I've made lemon cheesecake and I've got strawberries fresh from the market and…and King Island cream.'

'I'll help you clear away,' Jamie said, getting to his feet.

Bruno stood up as well, his voice a little gruff as he said, 'I'll give you a hand.'

Jamie gave him a slightly guarded smile. 'That'd be great. Thanks.'

'I help my mum all the time when I'm at home,' Bruno said as they left the room.

Patrizio put his hand under the dark, curly curtain of

Keira's hair, his fingers stroking the tension away as his eyes met hers. 'Are you OK?' he asked gently.

She pressed her lips together to stop them from trembling. 'I don't know… Sort of, I suppose…'

'Would you like me to speak to your father?' he asked.

Her shoulders went down in defeat. 'What would be the point? He's not going to change, not now. He's always had it in for me.'

Patrizio looked at the worried pleat of her brow and the shadows haunting her blue eyes. She had that little-girl-lost look again, which triggered all of his protective instincts all over again.

There were undoubtedly some disturbing undercurrents in this household, which he had not really noticed to this degree before. He had certainly been aware that things were not always rosy, but he had assumed it was merely a clash of wilful personalities, but now he was not so sure…

'I need some fresh air,' Keira said and pushed herself away from the table.

Patrizio accompanied her out to the patio, where the lights of the city blinked in the distance and the rattle and rumble of trams and trains sounded on the streets and tracks below.

He put his arms around her and held her close to him, breathing in the gardenia fragrance of her hair, his body instantly stirring as he felt her press herself closer.

It was getting harder and harder to keep her at a distance, he mused ruefully. With her so childlike and trusting in his arms like this, it was hard to think of her as the same person who had given herself to another man.

He didn't want to think of her as that person.

He wanted to think of her as his spirited but, at the same time, touchingly vulnerable wife, the woman he had wanted to spend the rest of his life with from the very first moment she had looked up at him at the boys' sports day and smiled at him so radiantly.

She had made a mistake, but then who hadn't? But, as she had said to his nephew the other night, it was hard to get through life without one or two regrets.

'Patrizio?' she murmured into the front of his shirt.

He tipped up her head with a finger beneath her chin. 'What is it, *cara*?' he asked.

Her eyes were like twin pools of dark blue water, their shimmering depths suddenly making it hard for him to breathe.

'Do you really think I'm a talented painter or were you just saying that?' she asked.

He brushed the pad of his thumb over the curve of her cheek. 'Is my good opinion so very important to you, Keira?'

The tip of her tongue came out briefly to moisten her lips, her eyes still connected to his. 'Yes…yes, it is.'

His eyes moved downwards to look at the soft contours of her mouth. 'I think you are very talented at many things,' he said, 'painting being just one of them.'

'What other things am I talented at?'

His lips curved upwards in a small smile as he brought his eyes back to hers. 'You are very talented at making me wonder why I am standing here at your parents' house when instead I could be in my own home in bed with your beautiful and sexy body writhing beneath me.'

'Oh…'

He touched her cheek again. 'You are blushing.'

'I'm hot.'

He smiled again and brought his mouth to just a whisper above hers. 'I know you are,' he said and pressed his mouth to hers.

Keira gave herself up totally to his kiss, the sensation of

his tongue probing for entry making her skin tingle all over in erotic anticipation. She pressed herself closer to his jutting erection, the hot hard heat of him thrilling her senses as she clung to him like a drowning person did to a rescuer.

'God, you make me so crazy for you,' he growled as he nibbled sensually at her bottom lip. 'I want to tear off your clothes right here and now, even though the whole of Melbourne is probably watching.'

Keira touched his tongue with hers in a flickering come-and-get me movement. 'I'm pretty crazy about you too,' she breathed.

He stroked his tongue against her bottom lip, back and forth, until her lips were buzzing with sensation and then, just when she thought she could stand it no more, he took her mouth again under the burning pressure of his, his tongue tangling with hers as one of his hands went to the gentle swell of her breast. She shivered as he pushed the shoulder strap of her dress aside so he could be skin on skin, her lack of a bra clearly delighting him if the deep sound he made in the back of his throat was any indication.

She arched her back as he brought his mouth to her breast, his teeth and tongue such an intimate torture on her quivering flesh that she hadn't registered they were no longer alone on the patio.

Patrizio suddenly lifted his head and, pulling her dress back into place, faced his nephew. 'Bruno, did you want me for something?' he asked.

Bruno's sneering gaze went to Keira's dishevelled state. 'No, but clearly *she* still does,' he said with a cynical curl of his lip.

Keira felt her face light up like a furnace and had to look away from that irritating smirk.

'But you're not the only one she wants,' Bruno continued coldly as he held out Keira's mobile phone to his uncle.

Keira felt her skin shrink all over her body, her heart thumping like a jackhammer in her chest as Patrizio took the phone from his nephew. She held her breath as he looked down at the text message on the screen, his jaw clenching as he read whatever was written there.

After what seemed an age, he flipped the phone shut and handed it to Keira with an unreadable look, before turning back to his nephew. 'I am not sure it is very wise to read or listen to other people's messages,' he said. 'There are instances when they can be easily misinterpreted and cause untold damage when in the wrong hands.'

'I warned you she's still seeing him,' Bruno said. 'Look at the guilt written all over her face.'

Keira lowered her gaze to the phone in her shaking hands and, with fumbling fingers, flipped open the screen and accessed her last received message. It was from Garth and, read out of context, was as damning as any could be.

Meet me Friday, four p.m. at my apartment—Garth.

She looked up to see Patrizio watching her. 'It's not what you think…' she said.

'No, I am sure it is not,' he said and, taking her arm, led her indoors back to the table, where Robyn had set out dessert and coffee.

The boys made short work of the cheesecake and strawberries but Keira could see that Patrizio had other things on his mind, even though he was making a valiant attempt to be polite and get through the generous helping of dessert Robyn had set before him.

'We will take the boys back to school on our way home,' he said to Robyn after everyone had finished.

'Thank you, Patrizio,' she said, blushing slightly. 'Kingsley's gone to bed with a headache. He's been under quite a bit of stress lately, as you can imagine.'

Keira felt like shaking her mother for always enabling her father to get away with his appalling behaviour. She exchanged rolled-eyed glances with Jamie and got to her feet. 'Don't make excuses for him, Mum,' she said. 'He's nothing but an overbearing tyrant who's been browbeating all of us for years. Why on earth do you put up with it?'

'Please don't cause any more trouble, Keira,' Robyn said. 'Haven't you done enough for one evening? Your father has an important meeting tomorrow and now he's unwell.'

Keira blew out her cheeks in frustration as she scooped up her purse. 'This is *such* a farce,' she said. 'You insist on playing happy families when you're as miserable as a wet weekend and have been for years.'

'I'm not miserable,' Robyn said. 'I love your father. He's a good man and stood by me when…' She paused and put an agitated hand up to her throat. 'I mean he's always stood by me.'

'Thank you for a lovely dinner, Mrs Worthington,' Patrizio said, coming between Keira and her mother. 'I will take Keira and the boys home. I apologise for Keira's behaviour; she is under a great deal of strain with her final exhibition coming up in less than four weeks.'

Robyn dabbed at her eyes. 'She should have become a teacher as we wanted,' she said. 'I hate to see her throw her life away after all I did for her…'

'Oh, for God's sake.' Keira rolled her eyes as she left the room.

Patrizio put his hand on Robyn's shoulder. 'Do not worry about her,' he said gently. 'I am looking after her now and will not let her throw her life away.'

Robyn looked up at him through eyes brimming with tears.

'He does love her, you know,' she choked. 'Kingsley, I mean. I admit he didn't for years…not until Jamie was born and looked just like her….he knew, then…'

Patrizio frowned, his chest suddenly feeling uncomfortably tight. 'Knew what?' he asked.

Robyn got to her feet and began clearing the dessert plates with jerky movements of her hands. 'I've had too much wine to drink,' she said, giving a forced laugh. 'Silly me, I've always been hopeless with alcohol. Keira's the same. More than half a glass and we can't remember a thing we've said or done.'

'Patrizio, are you taking us back or not?' Jamie asked from the door. 'We'll get a detention if we're not back by ten.'

'Coming,' Patrizio said over his shoulder.

Robyn gave him a sheepish look as she juggled the rest of the plates. 'Go on, Patrizio. I'll be fine…really.'

'Are you sure?'

She smiled a tremulous smile. 'Of course. I have to be, don't I? I'm a senator's wife.'

Patrizio's frown deepened as he went to where Keira and the boys were waiting for him. Bruno and Jamie were arguing about something that didn't sound particularly interesting or even very important. In fact he even had cause to wonder if their exchange of heated comments was genuine.

Keira, however, was staring into the darkness of the garden, her arms wrapped around her body as if she were cold, even though the bout of unusually warm spring weather had not yet abated.

'Time to go home?' he said as he brushed her bare shoulder with his hand.

She turned her head and, stripping her face of all emotion, followed him wordlessly to the car.

CHAPTER FIFTEEN

AFTER the boys were dropped off at school Patrizio let a few minutes of silence pass before he brought up the subject of the text message Keira had received. 'While it distresses me that my nephew took it upon himself to invade someone else's privacy in such a way, it raises the question in my mind as to whether or not you have been lying to me all this time about your continued relationship with Garth Merrick.'

'I haven't been lying to you,' she said. 'I haven't seen Garth for more than six or seven weeks.'

'But you have been in recent contact with him.'

She twisted her hands in her lap. 'Yes…I wanted to ask him about that night again. I thought it might help me remember something.'

He drew in a harsh breath. 'I can jog your memory if you like,' he said. 'You were lying in his bed with your body on show like a street—'

'Don't,' she said, pinching the bridge of her nose, her eyes clamped shut. 'Please don't.'

'It is true, Keira,' he went on ruthlessly. 'You claim you don't remember, but you did sleep with him. You said it yourself. There is no doubt of it.'

'I know…' she said in a strangled whisper. 'He told me too.'

He flicked a glance her way. 'Did he tell you how it happened? Who started it?'

She gave him a world-weary look. 'What difference does it make? You're never going to forgive me for it, so what does it matter who started it? It doesn't even matter to you that I can't remember doing it. As far as you're concerned, I betrayed you by sleeping with another man. You haven't even considered there might be another explanation.'

'What other explanation could there be?' he asked. 'I saw you in his bed, for God's sake.'

'Yes, I know, and I saw those photos that woman Rita Favore sent me, but it turned out that what I saw wasn't real,' she pointed out. 'What if there is some other explanation for what *you* saw?'

He brought the car to a halt in the driveway of his house, his dark gaze brooding. 'If there is another explanation I would like to know firstly what it is, and secondly who is going to give it to me, for apparently you cannot remember.'

'You think I'm lying about not remembering?' she asked in increasing distress. 'Do you realise how upsetting it is to wake up in one of your closest friend's bed and not remember a single detail of how you got there? *Do you?*'

Patrizio held her tortured gaze for several pulsing seconds, his mind going back over what Robyn Worthington had said earlier. 'Had you been drinking that night?' he finally asked.

She pressed her lips together and looked back at her hands. 'I had one or two sips of wine but I wasn't keen on it. I hardly ever drink—you should know that about me from when we were together before. I don't like the taste, for one thing, and I get a headache if I have more than one glass. I was very upset after we…we argued. I went to Garth's because I wanted to be with someone I trusted, someone who knew me and would look after me. I had the beginnings of a migraine and I knew if I didn't take something for it I would be out of it for days.'

'What did you take?'

She frowned, as if trying to remember. 'I'm not sure...Garth had something he'd been prescribed when he tore a ligament in his knee. It was pretty powerful, as I can remember feeling woozy a few minutes after taking it, but then that could have been the fact that I hadn't eaten for hours...'

His hands clenched the steering wheel as he tried to put out of his mind what he had seen that morning. 'So what you're saying is you have no recollection of what happened, no inkling of what led you to be in Merrick's bed?'

Keira shook her head silently.

'You said you were in no doubt that you slept with him,' he said, still clenching the steering wheel with white-knuckled force. 'Does that mean there was any evidence to suggest you had?'

She couldn't hold his gaze as she thought about the state of the bed that night. 'Yes...' she said. 'There was...'

She heard him release a ragged sigh as he opened the driver's door, watching as he came around to help her out of the car. She got out on legs that felt unsteady and followed him into the house, her heart aching all over again for what she had done to him.

He turned to face her once they were inside the house. 'This meeting you arranged with him for Friday,' he said. 'Are you telling me it was all above board? That you were only seeing him to search for answers?'

'Yes. He's moving to Canada in just over a month. He wasn't keen on seeing me when I called him, but he must have changed his mind.'

His dark eyes probed hers. 'I hope to God you are not lying to me, Keira,' he warned. 'If I find out you are, I will ruin you and your parents, and do not think I will not do it, for I will.'

She held his warning look for as long as she could. 'I'm not lying, Patrizio.' *Only a little bit.*

He let a few seconds pass before stating implacably, 'I do not want you to see him alone. In fact, I absolutely forbid it.'

Keira stared at him in dismay. 'But I have to see him alone! He would never agree to talk about that night with someone else present. He is really embarrassed about it, as I am too. It would be unthinkable to have someone listen in to such intimate details.' *Particularly the intimate details of her pregnancy*, she tacked on in mental anguish.

'If I do not accompany you then you do not go.'

'You can't dictate like that to me, Patrizio,' she said. 'I won't stand for it.'

The set to his mouth reeked of intransigence. 'You are my wife, Keira. I will not have you in another man's apartment without a chaperon present.'

She swung away from him in fury. 'I can't believe I'm hearing this,' she said. 'And I'm not your wife, remember? I am your soon-to-be ex-wife.'

His hand snaked out and turned her back to face him. 'You *are* my wife, Keira, and I intend for you to stay that way until such time as I am tired of you being so.'

Keira stared at him in outrage. 'What did you say?'

His eyes glinted with determination. 'I have decided our marriage will continue until I want it to finish.'

'You think you can *force* me to stay with you indefinitely?' she asked incredulously.

His sardonic smile answered for him.

'You're out of your mind,' she said, trying to pull away without success. 'This is total madness.'

'Perhaps it is, but it is very enjoyable madness, is it not?' he asked as he brought her closer. 'We might not be in love with each other but we are certainly still in lust with each other.'

'What is your mistress going to say when she hears you're staying with me for an indefinite period?' she asked with a pointed glare.

'She will have to accept it,' he returned smoothly.

'You don't give a toss for her or any other woman's feelings, do you? You think what you want is all that matters.'

'I want you, Keira, and yes—at this point in time that is all that matters to me.'

'You expect me to simply fit in with your plans like some sort of puppet?' she asked.

'I expect you to do what you think is in the best interests of the boys,' he said. 'They have five weeks left of school but then they have the difficult task of choosing which career path to follow. This seems to be more of an issue for your brother than my nephew. However, I believe if we stay together for as long as possible it will help them make the right choices.'

She looked at him through narrowed eyes. 'Why do I get the feeling you are milking this situation for all it's worth?'

He met her look with unwavering calm. 'I am merely doing what I can to make sure everyone gets what they want.'

She pursed her mouth. 'Yes, well, I can see you've made certain you're at the top of that list,' she said. 'You get exactly what you want—a chance to pay me back for being unfaithful.'

'Can you blame me for that?' he asked with an embittered glare. 'You threw our future away.'

'I wouldn't have done it if I had felt more secure in our relationship,' she argued.

'That is a preposterous thing to say,' he threw back angrily. 'I was working hard to build a solid base for our future. You should have realised that instead of acting like a spoilt child. I worshipped you, Keira. You were my whole life.'

Tears shone in her eyes. 'You were my life too…I loved you so much…' She took a gulping breath and added softly and brokenly, 'I still love you…'

His hands fell away from her as if she had burned him, his expression becoming mask-like. 'Then you have rather a strange way of showing it, agreeing to meet with your lover without my knowledge,' he said.

She lifted her tortured gaze to his. 'Do you feel anything for me, Patrizio? Anything at all, in spite of what I did?'

It was a moment or two before he answered and it was not the answer she had hoped for.

'If you are holding out for a declaration of love then you are going to be disappointed,' he said. 'I no longer have such feelings towards any woman and most particularly not for you. Ever since I found you had been unfaithful, all my relationships have been affairs of the body, not the heart. Thank you for the valuable lesson; fool that I am, I should have learned it long ago from my mother's example. She used my father in the way you did me. I stupidly thought it would never happen to me. I was wrong.'

Keira felt her spirits sink under the weight of her crushed hopes. 'I realise how bitter you are and I would be the same if the situation was reversed,' she said. 'But can't you find it in yourself to forgive me?'

His eyes hardened. 'No, I cannot.'

She swallowed the lump of pain in her throat. 'I guess there's no point in going on with this, then…'

'Is that why you gave yourself to me so willingly?' he asked after a taut pause. 'In an attempt to lure me back into your life on a more permanent basis?'

She looked at him in shock. 'No, of course not! I didn't want to see you any more than you wanted to see me and if it hadn't been for the boys I wouldn't have agreed to it.'

His dark gaze became suspicious. 'Did you cook this up with them?'

'What are you talking about?'

He gave a derisive laugh. 'Do not play the innocent with me, Keira. I am surprised I didn't guess it before now.'

'Guess what?'

His expression was full of contempt. 'You were not happy with how the divorce proceedings were going,' he said. 'So you decided to engineer a situation that would force us together long enough for me to recall how good we were together in an effort to soften me up when it came to pay out time.'

'That's not true! I didn't do anything of the sort!'

'I must admit I'm impressed with how you got Bruno onside,' he went on. 'He's certainly playing the role of the arrogant bully rather well, is he not?'

'I knew nothing about the boys' feud until my mother called,' she said. 'Jamie mentioned nothing to me and I'd only been speaking to him a day or two before.'

'Oh, come on, Keira,' he derided her. 'You expect me to believe that after tonight's little performance?'

She looked at him in confusion. 'What performance?'

'Bruno knew too much,' he said. 'He knew you had been in recent contact with Merrick; why else would he have mentioned your phone and then brought it to you with a message from your lover?'

'He must have guessed or something. He probably heard my phone beeping with a message in my purse and wanted to cause trouble.'

'He used to be very close to you,' Patrizio said. 'He spoke so highly of you until your affair. Up until then, he thought you were the best thing that had happened to me.'

Keira bent her head in shame. 'I know…'

'So you deny orchestrating the feud between the boys?' he said after he'd let another tense silence pass.

She brought her eyes back to his. 'Yes, of course I'm denying it. I was as surprised as you to find out they weren't getting on any more.'

He held her look for interminable seconds.

'I didn't do it, Patrizio,' she said. 'Why would I ask Bruno to insult me the way he has done? What good would that do if I had hopes of us getting back together permanently?'

'You think they have cooked it up themselves?' he asked with a frown.

She lowered her gaze again and chewed at her lip for a moment. 'I'm not sure…it's possible, I suppose…I know Jamie's been concerned about me lately.'

'Concerned? Why?'

She brought her eyes back to his briefly, before lowering them again. 'I've found it a bit hard to get on top of things lately. Finishing my thesis was hard and I was so ill after I got the flu I stayed in bed for ten days. I think Jamie thought it was depression more than anything.'

'And was it?' The tone of his voice had softened slightly.

Keira looked into his coal-black eyes and longed to tell him of how for weeks she had wanted to call him and beg him to take her back. She had even gone as far as dialling his number right up until the very last digit before her courage had failed her.

'Keira?' he prompted.

'A little bit, I guess,' she confessed, looking away again. 'A lot, actually…'

He let out a heavy sigh and raked a hand through his hair. 'I wish I had handled things differently.'

Her eyes flew back to his. 'What do you mean?'

'I don't think I knew you well enough back then,' he said.

'I rushed into marriage with you without stopping to think of how things would be for you with me away such a lot. I didn't realise how insecure it would make you feel. I think, in retrospect, we should have spent more time getting to know one another, like we are doing now.'

'Now?' she asked, blinking at him in surprise. 'You think we're getting to know each other now, the way things are?'

'Yes,' he answered. 'I have learned a lot about you lately.'

She swallowed again. 'L-like what?'

He held her gaze for a pulsing moment. 'You are not as wilful and rebellious as you make out. It is all a front to hide the very vulnerable, frightened person you really are inside. You kick out before someone else gets the chance to hurt you first.'

Keira captured her bottom lip and stayed silent.

'We have three weeks until the boys' exams,' he said. 'You also have your studies to complete, which I can see now has been rather difficult under the circumstances, so that is why I am proposing that we spend these next three weeks doing what we should have done when we first met. Learning to live together.'

She moistened her mouth with a nervous flicker of her tongue. 'How do you propose we do that?' she asked.

'Come here and I will show you,' he said, his dark eyes pulling her like a magnet.

Keira stepped towards him, her heart jumping as she felt his arms go around her, pulling her into his hard, solid warmth. She drew in an unsteady breath as his mouth came down on hers, the first touch of his lips sending her into a maelstrom of feeling.

He sought for entry and she gave it, her tongue flicking tentatively against his, heat exploding inside her at that first intimate contact. His hands went from her waist to cup her bottom, holding her tight against him, the hard ridge of his erection reminding her of the passion that still flared so heatedly between them. He no longer loved her but he desired her, which was the only compensation she could claim. It wasn't enough but it was better than nothing, which up until a few weeks ago was all she'd had. Almost two months of stark loneliness, the long arduous days without any contact with him apart from their lawyers. The long drawn-out divorce proceedings had been an attempt on her part to prolong the inevitable. She had wanted him to come storming round to confront her about her outrageous demands. She had longed to see him face to face, to tell him how sorry she was for what had happened, but he had never given her an opportunity.

Until now…

Patrizio lifted his mouth from hers. 'I think we should finish this in bed,' he said. 'Or do you have another preference?'

I would prefer it if you would love me, Keira thought as she shook her head. 'No, just being with you anywhere is enough.'

He looked down at her for endless moments, his dark eyes probing hers. 'You really do still love me, *cara*?'

She gave him a smile touched with sadness. 'Yes, I really do.'

'Then you will cancel your appointment with Merrick,' he said and, reaching for her purse, handed her the mobile phone. 'Text him now. Tell him you are not going to see him. Ever.'

Keira hesitated.

'Do it, Keira,' he commanded. 'If the press hears of you seeing your lover again it will blow our charade out of the water. Do it.'

She typed in the message and sent it, her expression still mutinous. 'Satisfied now?' she asked.

'Not completely,' he said as he scooped her up in his arms. 'But then the night is still young.'

CHAPTER SIXTEEN

PATRIZIO looked up from the morning paper when Keira came into the kitchen three weeks later. 'Are you not feeling well, *cara*?' he asked. 'You look pale and washed out.'

She gave him a quick on-off smile. 'I'm never very good in the morning, you know that.'

He rose from the stool and, cupping her face in his hands, pressed a kiss to her forehead. 'Look after yourself,' he said. 'You only have this week to get through before it will all be over.'

Keira felt her stomach clench in panic. 'W-what will be over?' she asked.

He smiled ironically. 'Have you forgotten about your final exhibition?'

'Oh…that…'

He tipped up her chin and searched her gaze. 'What is wrong? For the last few days you have seemed preoccupied. Have I done something to upset you?'

'No more than usual.' Actually that was unfair, Keira thought. The last three weeks he had been lovely towards her. She had almost fooled herself that he was falling in love with her again but if he was he hadn't said so. She had desperately wanted some clue to what he was feeling so she could tell him about her pregnancy but she was reluctant to destroy the fragile truce that had developed between them.

One of his brows slanted upwards. 'What is that supposed to mean?' he asked.

She pressed her lips together, frightened she was going to cry. 'I just want you to love me,' she said. 'Is that so much to ask?'

He stepped away from her, his expression closing over. 'Yes, it is.'

'Doesn't anything we've shared over the last three weeks mean anything to you?' she asked in desperation. 'We've been so happy together, you know we have.'

'Stop it, Keira,' he said. 'You know how this is going to work this time around.'

'But I don't want a divorce. How can you be so cruel?' She began to cry. 'Can't you see what this is doing to me?'

'You are emotional and highly stressed because of the exhibition,' he said. 'You will get over it.'

'Damn it! I'm emotional because I'm pregnant.'

Keira hadn't intended to tell him quite so bluntly. She saw the shock flash like lightning over his face and she bent her head, unable to hold his searing gaze.

'How many weeks are you?' he asked.

'I don't know for sure, but I haven't had a proper period for…for at least three months…'

The silence was so thick she could taste it when she ran her tongue across her dry lips.

'Is it mine?' The three words were like arrows through her heart.

She swallowed convulsively and dragged her eyes back to his. 'I'm…I'm not sure…but I think it's yours…' *Please God, let it be his*, she prayed.

She watched as his expression underwent various fleeting

changes: disbelief, cynicism and then a flicker of uncertainty, which he immediately masked.

'Is there any way of finding out for sure?' he asked.

She compressed her lips, trying to stop the tears that were burning at the back of her throat. 'Yes…I read up about it. An amniocentesis test is where they take a sample of amniotic fluid to establish paternity; it's also used to screen for problems with the baby, but there's a slight risk of miscarriage.'

He shoved a hand through his hair as he paced the room agitatedly. 'I will not have that on my head,' he bit out. 'If you had a miscarriage as a result of me insisting we find out who the father is, I will never forgive myself.'

He stopped pacing and swung back to look at her. 'What are you going to do?'

She looked at him worriedly. 'What do you mean, what am I going to do?'

'Are you going to have it or get rid of it?' he asked.

She swallowed deeply. 'You're…you're not suggesting I…I…terminate?'

'That is ultimately your decision, of course.'

'I don't want to do that…' she said. 'Please don't ask me to.'

'I am not going to ask you to do anything of the sort.'

'But you don't want this baby, do you?' she asked. 'Even if it turned out to be yours, you wouldn't want it, would you?'

'How long have you known you were pregnant?' he asked.

She bit her lip. 'I suspected it the week we started living together again, but I only did the test three weeks ago.'

He looked at her for a long time before responding. 'You have planned this rather well, haven't you, Keira? A brief reconciliation and then a declaration of undying love and the somewhat belated announcement of your pregnancy to force my hand to keep you in my life permanently.'

'I didn't plan any of this.'

'I must say I find that very hard to believe,' he said. 'Why didn't you tell me you were pregnant as soon as you found out? You've had plenty of opportunities to do so.'

'I was worried about how you would react.'

'Burying your head in the sand is not the way to handle a situation like this, Keira. You must have known you were pregnant long before we began our reconciliation.'

'I put it down to being ill with the flu,' she said. 'I sort of lost track of where I was in my cycle. That must be how I fell pregnant in the first place. I know we used condoms when I forgot to take my pills regularly but everyone knows they're not foolproof. We skated on thin ice plenty of times, if you remember.'

Patrizio did remember. How could he forget how she had felt in the shower, her body all lathered with soap, his body probing her from behind, so tempted to fill her with his pumping release but pulling back just in time? God, his belly was crawling with desire, here and now, just thinking about it. She had turned around in the shower stall and taken matters into her own hands and mouth.

His eyes went to her mouth, his groin thickening as he imagined her soft pouting lips surrounding him, her violet-blue gaze sultry as she…

He gave himself a mental shake. She had probably done the very same with Garth Merrick, taking him any way she could to feed her insatiable desire for pleasure. He could see it in her eyes now, that hungry look that smouldered there almost constantly.

'I will not accept that child as mine until I have proof,' he said.

Keira felt her control slipping. 'I can't believe you're being so heartless,' she said. 'Do you realise what this is like for me?'

'I realise you are worried about your future.'

'This is not about money, for God's sake!'

'Then what is it about?'

'It's about us…you and me and…and the baby.'

'You have got it all mapped out, haven't you?'

She turned away in anger. 'It wasn't supposed to be like this…That's why I waited as long as I could to tell you. I wanted to tell you when things had settled down…I wanted you to be pleased…I wanted you to be happy…' *I wanted you to love me and our baby no matter who its father is*, she added silently.

'You are asking too much, Keira,' he said coldly.

'Yes, I am, aren't I?' she said through glittering tears. 'You don't love me any more and you never will.'

Patrizio watched as she turned away and left the room, the words to call her back sticking like thorns in his throat.

'Signor Trelini left a message for you,' Marietta said later that day. 'He said he had to fly to Sydney on business and might not be back until after your exhibition opens.'

'Oh…'

'Don't be too disappointed, Keira,' Marietta said. 'He will show his support in some other way, I am sure.'

Keira wasn't so sure about that. 'The least he could have done is tell me himself,' she said dispiritedly.

The housekeeper tilted her head at her. 'Have you told him you are expecting a child?'

Keira blinked at her in surprise. 'How did you know I was pregnant?'

Marietta folded her arms in a smug pose. 'I have had four children. You think I do not know the signs by now? Besides, your sweaters were in such a mess I had to refold them all. I found the test.'

Keira let out a long sigh and sat down. 'I've told him but I don't think he's taking the news all that well.'

'He is probably nervous about being a father,' Marietta said. 'My husband was the same, but do not worry, he will be overcome with joy once it hits home.'

She gave the housekeeper a strained smile. 'I certainly hope so.'

Marietta patted her on the shoulder. 'He just needs a bit more time. Be patient with him.'

Keira read something in the older woman's gaze that alerted her to the fact that Marietta knew more about Patrizio than she did herself.

'He loves you, Keira,' the housekeeper said. 'He just does not realise it yet.'

Keira felt her heart swell with hope. 'You think so?'

'I know he does,' Marietta said with that same smug smile in place. 'Why else would he fly to Sydney on business and stay away longer than necessary? He is, how you say it…regrouping? He has to recharge the batteries of his resolve to keep you at a distance. He does not want to make another mistake but he will realise soon the biggest mistake he made was to let you go.'

'So you've known all along that our reconciliation is a sham?'

'Listen, Keira, I am the wife of an Italian man and the mother of his four sons. What I do not know about Italian men isn't worth knowing. Signor Trelini is very proud. He refused to mention what happened back then, even though it was all over the papers day after day. He gritted his teeth and carried on as if everything was normal but inside he has been simmering with anger. Having you back in his life has forced him to confront his feelings. He is not going to give in without a fight, let me tell you.'

'What do you think I should do?' Keira asked.

'Love him,' Marietta said. 'That is all you can do. Love him to bits.'

Keira smiled in spite of her sagging spirits. 'You really are much more than a housekeeper, aren't you?' she said.

Marietta's dark brown eyes twinkled. 'You had better believe it.'

'Guess what?' Harriet Fuller rushed up to Keira on the opening night of the exhibition.

'What?'

'All of your paintings have a sold sticker on them,' Harriet informed her excitedly. 'Every single one.'

Keira's startled gaze went to where her works were displayed. It was true. Each one had been sold. She swung her gaze back to her friend. 'Do you know who bought them?' she asked.

'That man over there,' she said, pointing to a man of about forty or so who was signing a credit card slip. 'Do you know him?'

Keira hadn't realised how much she had hoped it was Patrizio who had bought her paintings until she saw that it was not. The man was totally unfamiliar to her. 'No,' she said, turning back to Harriet. 'I don't know him. What is he, an art collector or something?'

'I don't know,' Harriet said. 'But who cares? You've caused such a sensation the press want an interview and the arts council representative wants to do a feature article on you in their next newsletter.'

Keira couldn't help but be caught up in the excitement but as the evening went on she began to flag with tiredness. She scanned the crowd several times, hoping for the sight of a tall, dark figure but was disappointed each time.

'Didn't your husband or parents make it?' Harriet asked towards the end of the evening.

Keira shook her head sadly. 'No. Patrizio was called away on business. And, as for my parents…Well, this is definitely not their scene. My father would be concerned that he was going to be mingling with drug addicts or something and thereby permanently tarnish his reputation.'

'Better not tell him about Devlin Prosserton, then,' Harriet advised, jerking her head towards one of the more infamous students, who had a reputation for partying rather hard.

'Yes, I guess not,' Keira agreed and, blowing out a sigh added wearily, 'I'm bushed. I think I'll head home and sleep for a week.'

'Well, at least you can sleep knowing there's money in the bank,' Harriet said. 'Just think—you won't have to die after all. You're already famous.'

Keira stretched her mouth into a smile. 'Yeah, how about that, so I am.'

'You have a visitor, Keira,' Marietta announced the following day. 'She is waiting in the lounge.'

Keira went downstairs to find her mother sitting on the edge of one of the leather sofas, her fingers twisting the strap of her handbag agitatedly. 'Mum, what a surprise. I was going to visit you today as I wanted to tell you—'

'Keira…' Robyn got to her feet. 'Wait, please, I have something to tell you first.'

Keira put a hand up to her throat. 'Is Dad OK?'

'Yes…yes, of course he is. He's fine…just fine…'

'What, then?'

Robyn removed yet another layer of coral lipstick from her lips with a nervous movement of her tongue. 'Keira, I have a confession to make.'

Keira stood very still, her palms moistening in mild panic. Her mother's normally well groomed figure seemed to have an element of disarray about it; her shoes and handbag didn't match and Keira noticed that one of her mother's painted nails was chipped when she put her hand up to her throat in a gesture of discomfiture.

'I have been so critical of you with regard to your affair with Garth,' Robyn said with a grimace of remorse contorting her features. 'It's very hypocritical of me because I once did the very same thing to your father when we were first married.'

Keira's eyes opened wide. 'You did?'

Robyn nodded, her cheeks going pink. 'I had a brief fling with an old friend…He was an artist.'

This time it was Keira's turn to moisten her dry lips. 'You mean…you mean I'm not Dad's daughter?'

'You *are* his daughter, Keira, there's no doubt about it,' Robyn said. 'I must admit I was a bit uncertain at first but after a while I just knew you were his. Your father was furious with me, as you can imagine, but he took me back and nurtured me through a very difficult pregnancy. I will always love him for that.'

'But he doesn't love me.'

'That's not true,' Robyn insisted. 'Oh, he's a stubborn old goat, of course, and it took him years to accept you were his, which meant he was often a little distant towards you. He realised his mistake when Jamie was born. You were so alike, but I guess by then it was too late. He didn't know how to be a loving father to you. He wasn't used to being affectionate towards you.'

Keira frowned. 'Why are you telling me this now?'

'I wanted to clear the air between us,' Robyn said. 'I know we haven't had the greatest mother-daughter relationship there is, which is probably more my fault than yours. I felt so guilty about what I'd done that it made it hard for me to stand up for myself all these years. I didn't stand up for you either. I was so very grateful to your father for not divorcing me that I didn't want to rock the boat. But I've been thinking a lot about you lately. I guess that's really why I am here telling you this now. I don't want you to make the same mistake with Patrizio that I made with your father. Patrizio's a strong man and a very determined and proud one.'

'Yes…yes, he is.'

'You are happy with him, aren't you, darling?' Robyn asked. 'I've been so worried about you. I don't want you to get hurt.'

'Oh, Mum,' Keira said, hugging her mother to her tightly. How she wished she could tell her she was in a similar situation with regard to her pregnancy!

Robyn began to shake with sobs. 'I have been such a terrible mother to you. I can't seem to get it right, no matter what I do.'

'It's all right, Mum.' Keira stroked her mother's back. 'I'm just glad we've been able to talk about it now.'

Robyn dabbed at her eyes with a tissue. 'You told me you had something to tell me,' she said, stuffing the tissue up her sleeve. 'What is it?'

Keira took an unsteady breath and announced, 'I'm pregnant.'

'Oh, my darling girl,' Robyn said, reaching for her again. 'I am so happy for you. It's exactly what you and Patrizio need to bring you even closer together. Have you told him yet?'

'Yes, she has,' Patrizio said from the door.

Keira turned from her mother's embrace to look at him. 'I—I didn't realise you were coming back today…'

'Come here, *cara*, and give me a kiss,' he commanded. 'Your mother will not be offended, will you, Mrs Worthington?'

'Of course not and please do stop calling me that,' Robyn said, flushing slightly. 'Robyn's my name.'

'Robyn, then,' Patrizio said and bent down to press a brief but firm kiss to Keira's mouth. 'How are you feeling?'

'Fine…'

'I'd better get going,' Robyn said. 'Kingsley will be wondering where I've got to.'

'I'll walk you out,' Keira said.

'No need to do that, darling,' her mother said. 'You and Patrizio need some time together. I'll see myself out.'

Once her mother had left, Keira eased herself out of Patrizio's hold. 'You should have told me you were coming home today,' she said. 'I gave Marietta the night off. There are only leftovers to eat.'

'Shouldn't you be eating more than leftovers?' he asked.

'I thought you would be happy if I faded away to a shadow,' she said. 'That would make things easier for you, wouldn't it?'

'How so?'

'You could be rid of me and the baby. That's what you want, isn't it?'

'You seem to be very certain of that.'

She looked at him searchingly. 'Have you changed your mind?'

He held her gaze for several moments. 'I have been doing some thinking while I was away,' he said. 'I am prepared to continue with our marriage indefinitely for the sake of our child.'

'So you're admitting there's a very real possibility it could be yours?' she asked.

'I would prefer to have it confirmed but I realise this is a difficult time for you and I am offering my support, particularly as Merrick is leaving the country within a week or so.'

She thinned her lips and swung away. 'You won't let it go, will you?'

'I am sorry,' he said after a tense pause. 'I should not have said that, especially when I know for a fact you have not seen Merrick while I have been out of town.'

Keira turned around to look at him. 'How do you know I haven't seen him?'

His dark, unfathomable gaze secured hers. 'Because I have had someone tailing you while I was away.'

'You've what?' she choked.

'It was within my interests to make sure you were not tempted to stray,' he said. 'I wanted to see if you were as good as your word.'

Keira began to seethe with rage, and clenching her fists, glared at him. 'How dare you? How *dare* you put me to the test like that?'

'I dared because I want to make sure you are as committed to this marriage as I am this time around,' he said. 'And I will continue to keep tabs on you until such time as trust is re-established.'

'It will never be re-established as I'm not going to be a part of such a farce,' she threw at him furiously. 'Once this week is over and the boys are through their exams I'm leaving and I'm never coming back.'

His mouth tightened. 'You will not be going anywhere without my permission,' he said intractably.

She gave him a mutinous glare. 'You just watch me.'

His hands came down on to the tops of her shoulders. 'You are the most maddening woman I have ever met,' he growled. 'I came back determined to set things right between us and you are doing everything in your power to ruin what we have.'

'What is it we actually have?' she asked. 'Bitterness, regret and not much else.'

'That is not true,' he argued. 'We still have the attraction we have always felt for each other.'

'But it's so empty without love to sustain it,' she said. 'Don't you see that?'

'You claim to love me. Perhaps, in time, I will learn to love you again.'

'There is no guarantee you will though, is there?'

'Life does not come with a whole list of guarantees, Keira,' he said. 'No one can predict the future. If anyone had told me even five weeks ago that I would be standing in front of you tonight, desperate to make love to you, I would have laughed in their face, but here I am, fighting not to drag you into my arms and have you right here on the floor at our feet.'

Keira felt her chin give a little wobble. 'You really mean that?'

He smiled and pulled her into his arms, burying his head into her wavy hair. 'I have been thinking of nothing else for the last seven days,' he said. 'I have missed you so much, *tesoro mio*.'

'I've missed you too,' she said into his chest. 'I was hoping you would make it back for my exhibition but…' She let out a despondent sigh.

He looked down at her. 'I intended to get back in time, in spite of the message I left with Marietta, but at the last minute one of the accountants found a slight discrepancy in the figures in the report we were looking over so I had to see to it right then and there. I am sorry I wasn't back in time but I sent someone on my behalf, did he not tell you?'

Keira blinked up at him once or twice. 'No…should he have?'

'I instructed him to buy everything you had painted,' he said. 'The very least he could have done was to tell you so.'

'Oh…so it *was* you…'

'Of course it was me, *cara*,' he said. 'I have a lot of luxury homes to decorate, no? I thought it would be a good way to get your name out there.'

'It was very good of you, considering how you feel about me…'

He brought up her chin with one finger. 'And do you know how I feel about you?' he asked.

She let out a shaky sigh. 'I'm not sure I want to even think about it in case I'm disappointed.'

'I feel like holding you in my arms for as long as I can,' he said. 'I want to breathe in your scent, to taste you, to feel you convulsing around me. I have been thinking about it the whole time I was away. No one completes me the way you do.'

But you don't love me, Keira thought as she gave herself up to his kiss. But then she recalled the housekeeper's words: Love him. Love him to bits.

That would be the easy part.

CHAPTER SEVENTEEN

'How do you think your last exam went?' Keira asked Jamie at the end of the following week.

'I'm just glad they're all over,' he said, rotating his straw in his milkshake.

'How are things with Bruno?' she asked.

'He's been really good the last few days,' he said, still looking at the movements of the straw. 'As soon as he heard you were pregnant, he kind of figured things must be on the level with you and Patrizio.'

'That's a relief,' she said. 'But I still can't work out why you didn't say something earlier about what was going on between you both. Why didn't you?'

He gave her a shamefaced look and twirled his straw again. 'We-ll…'

Keira gave him a probing glance. 'What's going on, Jamie?'

'I'm not supposed to tell you.'

'Tell me what?'

Jamie met her gaze, a rueful smile twisting his mouth. 'It's true Bruno and I had a bit of a cooling off when you and Patrizio first broke up. Bruno said some pretty horrible things about you but then so did I about his uncle. But we sorted it out after a while. We weren't as good mates as before, I guess, because we both felt a conflict of loyalties but we were never really feuding, or at least not enough to get expelled.'

Keira's mouth fell open. 'You mean it was all an act?'

He gave her a sheepish look. 'Yep.'

She sat back in her seat. 'Whose idea was it? Yours or his?'

'Neither,' he answered.

She leaned forward again. 'Whose, then?'

His eyes moved away from hers. 'I'm not supposed to tell. I promised.'

Keira grabbed his wrist and dug her fingers in. 'You have to tell me, Jamie. Was it Patrizio?'

He shook his head.

She frowned. 'Was it Mum?'

He shook his head again.

'Dad?'

'No, and stop asking as I'm not going to tell.'

She let his wrist go and drummed her fingers on the table. 'I can't think who else would set you up to do it,' she said, still frowning. 'It wasn't as if anyone else had any reason to intervene. Patrizio and I were in the throes of a divorce. We were just weeks away from agreeing on a settlement date…'

'Someone obviously didn't want you to go through with it,' Jamie said. 'They thought that if you were forced to see each other to discuss what was going on between Bruno and me, you would both realise what you were throwing away.'

'But who?' she asked. 'Why can't you tell me? It's so important, Jamie.'

'Why is it important?' he asked. 'You're back together now; that's all that matters, surely?'

Keira decided to come clean. The boys were through their exams. Besides, she was sick to death of pretending to be so happy when she was so very miserable. 'Jamie,' she said, reaching for his hand again. 'Listen to me. Bruno was right. Patrizio and I are not genuinely reconciled. Your little prank didn't work.'

Jamie stared at her open-mouthed. 'But…but you said you're pregnant!'

She could feel her face heating. 'Yes but…but it might not be Patrizio's…'

His throat moved up and down. 'You're not thinking of…you know…getting rid of it, are you?'

'I want this baby more than anything. The poor little thing is not to blame for any of this. I just want Patrizio to love me in spite of what's happened, but he doesn't.'

Jamie's brows met over his eyes. 'But that's not true, Keira. He does love you. I'm sure of it.'

She shook her head sadly. 'He doesn't, Jamie. He told me. He has never forgiven me for that night. And now, with this complication, I don't think he ever will.'

'So what are you going to do?'

She let out a long jagged sigh. 'I don't know…He's offered to stay married to me for the sake of the baby but I don't want to live with a man who doesn't trust me. That would be soul-destroying.'

'Like Mum has done?'

Keira's eyes went to her brother's. 'You know about what happened all those years ago?'

He nodded. 'I overheard them arguing about it a few weeks back. It was after you'd been over for a visit during the holidays. I was going to mention it to you but you were going through a pretty rough time with the divorce and all. I didn't want to add to your stress.'

She gave another weary sigh. 'It all makes sense now, you know, the way Dad has always been so critical of me. I guess he's been looking for signs that I wasn't his. I dread the same thing happening with my baby.'

'But it could be Patrizio's, right?' Jamie said.

'Yes, but he's hedging his bets until the ultrasound and we have a little more idea about the dates. I have an appointment with the obstetrician and he said he'd come with me.'

Jamie tapped at his lips thoughtfully. 'Have you told Garth about the pregnancy?'

'Yes.'

'What was his reaction?'

'He said he didn't think it could be his.'

Jamie looked at her for two or three beats of silence before saying, 'So now you have to find a way to convince Patrizio that he's the father.'

'Yeah, like what?' Keira answered in despair. 'The only way to do that would be to rewrite the past and have me totally innocent of sleeping with another man, but that's not likely to happen, is it?'

Jamie didn't answer but when Keira looked back at him he was frowning, his blue eyes staring into the distance as if he were mulling over something in his mind that didn't quite make sense.

'Jamie?'

He gave himself a shake and looked back at her. 'Sorry, Kiki. What were you saying?'

She reached for the bill for their snack. 'Nothing important,' she said. 'Come on. I have to get home. Patrizio is having his sister Gina and Bruno over for dinner and I don't want to be late.'

Keira was upstairs dressing for dinner when she felt the first cramp in her abdomen. She stood very still, hoping she was imagining it. She looked at her reflection in the mirror above the basin, shocked at how pale and drawn her features looked.

After a few minutes her stomach settled and she put the finishing touches to her make-up before joining Patrizio downstairs.

He looked up from the drinks tray Marietta had laid out in preparation for the evening. 'Are you all right, Keira?' he asked with a concerned frown.

She pasted a bright smile on her face. 'Yes, of course,' she said. 'I'm sorry I was so long getting ready. I didn't realise the time when I took Jamie out for a milkshake.'

'How is he?' he asked, handing her a tall glass of bubbling mineral water.

'Very relieved the exams are over.'

'Yes, I imagine he is,' he said. 'Bruno said the same when I spoke to him earlier today.'

Keira licked her lips nervously. 'Patrizio…there's something you should know about the boys' feud.'

He looked at her with interest. 'Oh, really? What?'

'They had cooled off their friendship after we separated but not to the point of jeopardising their education. Someone suggested they work at bringing us back together by pretending to be enemies.'

'Did he tell you who the someone was?'

'No, he said he'd promised not to.'

His frown brought his brows together. 'Have you any idea who it might have been?'

'No idea at all,' she answered. 'Do you?'

He rubbed at his jaw for a moment or two. 'The only person I can think of is Marietta,' he said. 'She's always been very fond of you. She never agreed with me going ahead with the divorce and she refused to remove your things from the house.'

'You think she would go to such lengths to set up something like this? You could have fired her for interfering in your personal life.'

'We can ask her if you like.'

Marietta came in with a platter of nibbles as if on cue. 'Did you want to ask me something?'

'Yes, Marietta,' Patrizio said. 'Did have anything to do with Bruno and Jamie's supposed feud?'

'No, of course not.'

'Are you sure?'

Marietta put her hands on her generous hips. 'Listen, Signor Trelini, I might think you were a fool for not giving Signora Trelini a second chance but meddling in other people's marriages is not my preferred choice of hobby.'

'Thank you, Marietta,' Patrizio said. 'That will be all for now.'

Marietta smiled at Keira as she left the room.

Patrizio waited until the housekeeper had gone before he asked, 'Do you believe her?'

'I have no reason not to,' she answered. 'If she said she didn't do it, she didn't.'

'Maybe she has forgotten.'

Keira turned away at his words, her mouth pulled tight. 'Yes, maybe she has.'

Patrizio came over to her and touched her on the shoulder. 'That was crass of me. I am sorry.'

She turned around and faced him. 'This is never going to work, is it? You and me and our history. It's going to ruin the baby's life, growing up with you throwing asides at me all the time. You have to let it go or let me go. Make your choice.'

He ran his hands down the length of her arms to encircle both of her wrists. 'Keira, there's something I want to say to you before my sister and nephew arrive. I have wanted to say it for days.'

Keira held her breath, her heart beginning to thump inside her chest wall. The earnestness in his dark gaze made her wonder if he had changed his mind about her. 'What is it?' she asked, her voice so soft it came out more like a breathless whisper.

The doorbell sounded and Patrizio rolled his eyes in frustration. 'Why is it that my wife is always late and my sister is always early?' He put her from him with a rueful smile. 'We will have to have this talk later, after they have left.'

Marietta came bustling in with Gina and Bruno. 'Signor Trelini, your sister and nephew are here,' she said with a smile.

'Thank you, Marietta.'

'Hello, Keira,' Gina said, rushing over to kiss Keira on both cheeks. 'It is truly wonderful to see you. I am so pleased you and Patrizio have withdrawn the petition for a divorce.'

'Thank you, Gina. It's lovely to see you too.'

'It's great news about your pregnancy,' Gina said. 'How are you feeling?'

Keira did her best to ignore the slight twinge of pain deep and low in her abdomen. 'I'm a bit tired but that's to be expected.'

'Bruno, say hello to your aunt,' Gina prompted.

Bruno stepped forward, his expression more than a little sheepish. 'Hello, Keira,' he said, shuffling from foot to foot.

'It's all right,' she said in an undertone as Gina moved across the room to take a drink off her brother. 'Jamie told me what was going on.'

'I'm sorry if I overplayed it a bit,' Bruno said. 'I wanted to make sure my uncle believed it was real.'

'You were very convincing,' she said. 'But I meant what I said that night we went out for a meal. We all make mistakes in life and the one I made is one I will always regret.'

'Uncle Patrizio has forgiven you so that is all that matters,' he said. 'I am prepared to do the same.'

'Thank you,' she said. 'I really appreciate it, Bruno.'

Patrizio raised his glass in a toast as he came to join them. 'To the end of the academic year,' he said.

Keira reached for her glass where she had placed it on the coffee table but she crumpled to the floor when a lightning bolt of pain ripped through her belly.

'Keira!' Patrizio was on his knees beside her within seconds, his face contorted with worry. 'What's the matter?'

She clutched at her stomach, panic widening her eyes. 'I think I'm losing it…'

'The baby?'

She nodded and bit down hard on her lip to stop herself from crying out in agony.

'I'll call an ambulance,' Gina said, rushing to the phone, calling out to Marietta on the way, 'Marietta! Get some towels quickly.'

Patrizio carried Keira to a small bedroom off the study, his face paling when he saw the blood on his hands from where he had been supporting her. 'Oh, dear God…'

Keira closed her eyes, trying to breathe through the clawing contractions that signalled the end of her baby's life before it had even had a chance to begin. 'Oh, no…' she gasped. 'This is all my fault. I've caused this to happen. I know I have…'

'Shh, *cara*,' he soothed her gently, wiping her clammy brow. 'Do not talk. We will get you to hospital as soon as we can. Be strong, *tesoro mio*. Be strong, my darling. Be strong.'

Keira vaguely registered the wail of a siren in the distance before she felt her grip on consciousness begin to slip out of her reach. Patrizio's features blurred in front of her; his dark eyes looked like bullet holes in the snow, so white was his face. She reached up with a trembling hand and touched his face to see if he was really there beside her, looking and sounding as if he cared for her more than life itself.

Patrizio covered her hand with his and brought it to his mouth, his voice breaking over the words. 'Forgive me, *cara.* Forgive me for being such a stubborn fool. I don't want to lose you. I could not bear to lose you permanently.' But he wasn't sure if she had heard him. Her eyelids had fluttered and closed, her breathing became increasingly shallow and her face was the colour of marble just as the ambulance officers arrived.

The doctor came out to where Patrizio was pacing the waiting room with his sister and nephew watching from the sidelines. 'Mr Trelini?'

'How is she?' Patrizio asked, his face ashen with dread.

'She is fine and so is the baby,' Dr Channing said. 'Your wife is sixteen weeks pregnant so she should be out of the danger zone in another week or two. I thought she was going to lose it but the bleeding stopped and as long as she has plenty of bed rest for the next week or two things should progress normally.'

Patrizio stood dumbly in front of the doctor, his face draining of colour.

The doctor peered at him. 'Are you all right?'

Patrizio swallowed the painful lump in his throat, his chest feeling as if an industrial-sized clamp were on it. 'Yes...yes, I'm fine. I just didn't realise she was that...' he gulped again '...that far along.'

'Yes, well, first pregnancies are often like that, especially when the mother has continued taking oral contraceptives during the first few weeks. It's a bit hard to establish dates until an ultrasound is performed.'

'Can I see her?'

'She is still slightly sedated,' Dr Channing said. 'But yes, you can see her. She hasn't been well for some time, apparently. Her bloods showed she had been exposed to one or two nasty viruses. Has she had flu-like symptoms recently?'

Patrizio felt ashamed that he hadn't realised how unwell she had been and how he had probably contributed to it with his bullish demands. 'Yes, she has,' he answered.

'Her iron stores are low,' the doctor told him. 'I considered giving her a transfusion but with proper nutrition and adequate rest she should bounce back quite quickly. The first trimester of pregnancy is often fraught with these sorts of difficulties.'

'Thank you,' Patrizio said. 'I will take good care of her.'

The doctor smiled. 'She's a very lucky girl,' he said. 'I see far too many women in here without loving partners to support them through times such as this. I wish you both well.'

Patrizio felt the doctor's words tear through his chest like a viciously sharp blade. He had not supported Keira when she had needed it most. She had been at least two weeks pregnant the night of their horrendous argument, no doubt the fluctuating hormones of early pregnancy adding to her emotionally charged state.

'We're going home,' Gina said, touching him on the arm. 'If there's anything we can do, just let us know.'

He looked down at his sister and nephew and somehow managed to stretch his mouth into the semblance of a smile. 'Thank you for being with me tonight. I really appreciate it.'

'It was no trouble,' Gina said. 'But it's you she needs right now.'

He let out an uneven sigh as he turned towards the intensive care unit. 'I know.'

Patrizio was shocked all over again at Keira's pallor. She looked as if every drop of blood had been drained out of her.

He took one of her limp hands in his and brought it up to his mouth, fighting back tears as he contemplated a future without her. What did it matter if she had betrayed him? She had only done it the once and it had probably been a knee-jerk reaction to what she had suspected he was getting up to in her absence.

Rita Favore was still up to her tricks; only that day he had heard of another man she was targeting with her aggressive seduction techniques. He should have seen it coming and done something to stop it; instead he had ignored it at his peril.

'Keira? Can you hear me?' he asked.

She murmured something unintelligible but didn't open her eyes.

'I love you, *tesoro mio*,' he said, stroking her face with his fingers. 'I have been such a fool. I have never stopped loving you.'

'Garth?'

Patrizio froze.

'Is that you?' she said, moving her head back and forth on the pillow, her eyes still closed. 'I've been waiting for you…'

Patrizio released her hand and got to his feet, his chest feeling so constricted he couldn't draw in a breath. She was deeply unconscious and yet the first person she had called out for was Garth Merrick. Didn't that tell him all he needed to know? He was never going to be the person she turned to when things got her down.

'Is everything all right?' the nurse on duty asked as she picked up the chart off the end of the bed.

He gave himself a mental shake and brushed past her to leave. 'Yes,' he said brusquely. 'Everything is just fine.'

CHAPTER EIGHTEEN

KEIRA woke to the sound of a cheery nurse at the end of her bed. 'Mrs Trelini, your parents are here. Do you feel up to seeing them or would you like me to send them away?'

She dragged herself upright, wincing as her body protested at the movement. 'It's OK,' she said. 'Send them in.'

'Oh, my poor little darling,' Robyn said as she rushed to Keira's bedside and enveloped her in a gentle hug. 'Patrizio called us and told us you were in hospital. He was so distraught. Are you all right? How is the baby?'

'We're both OK, Mum,' Keira said, holding her mother's hand tightly.

Her father stepped forward, his throat rising and falling as he put a hand on her shoulder. 'Keira…' He swallowed again. 'I have been such a fool. Your mother and I have had a long talk. I don't know what to say…other than I love you and hope you get better soon.'

Keira reached for him and was comforted by the warmth of his embrace, deeply moved too by the moisture she saw in his eyes as he eventually straightened.

'When are they letting you come home?' her mother asked.

'I'm not sure; tomorrow, I think.'

'We'll leave you to rest,' her father said. 'Patrizio is waiting outside. Call us if you need anything. And, when you feel well enough, we'll have you both over for a barbecue or something.'

Keira smiled at her father. 'That would be nice, Dad.'

He bent down and kissed the top of her head. 'Take care of yourself, princess.'

'I will…'

Patrizio's expression was haggard and his dark gaze looked shadowed with weariness as he came to stand beside the bed after her parents had left. 'I thought you were going to die,' he said. 'I cannot forgive myself for not looking after you properly.'

Keira reached for his hand and laid it across her belly. 'It's yours, Patrizio,' she said softly. 'The baby is yours.'

'I know,' he said, swallowing deeply. 'The doctor told me you are four months pregnant. Can you forgive me for my part in what has happened?'

She blinked back tears. 'There's nothing to forgive,' she said. 'You didn't do anything wrong. That was me, remember?'

He removed his hand and began to pace the room but the space was too limited for anything more than a stride or two before he had to turn. He reminded Keira of a caged jungle cat, frustrated and restless to be free.

He swung back to face her, his coal-black eyes misty. 'I want to call off the divorce but I must insist that you promise you will never see, speak of or even mention Garth Merrick ever again.'

She began to pluck at the sheet covering her body. 'If that is what you want.'

'I absolutely demand it, Keira,' he said. 'I do not want to live the rest of our lives with the shadow of his presence hanging over us.'

'I understand…'

'I am not prepared to let you go a second time,' he said, his voice tripping over the words. 'I love you too much.'

Keira took an uneven breath as a little hammer of doubt began to tap inside her head. 'Are you only saying this now because you know the baby is yours?' she asked, looking at him with a slightly narrowed gaze.

His brows moved together. 'Of course not. How can you ask that?'

'You always insisted you didn't love me any more,' she answered. 'You also insisted you could never forgive me, that I had permanently ruined our marriage.'

He shoved a hand through his already messy hair. 'I know what I said back then, but the truth is I want you back.'

She plucked at the hem of the sheet again. 'Because of the baby…'

'Even if it wasn't my baby I would have taken you back,' he insisted. 'I was about to tell you that last night when Gina and Bruno arrived.'

Keira wanted to believe him but how could she be sure? Things hadn't really changed between them, in spite of what he said. The fact that he was forbidding her to ever mention Garth's name suggested he hadn't and never would forgive her for what she had done.

'We can make ours a good marriage if we work at it, Keira,' he said into the silence. 'Things are different now. My business is well established. I don't have to travel as much and if I do you and the baby can come with me.'

'Do you really love me?' she asked in a tiny voice.

He sat on the edge of the bed and picked up her hand and brought it to his mouth. 'I adore you, *cara*. I need you. I have been out of my mind with worry the last few hours, thinking I was going to lose you for ever. It made me realise what lies

I have been telling myself. There I was, accusing you of always burying your head in the sand, but I have been doing the very same thing.'

Tears shone in her eyes as he kissed each of her fingertips. 'I can't wait to come home and be your wife again,' she said.

He gave her hand another tender squeeze. 'I spoke to the doctor while your parents were here. He said you can come home in the morning.'

When Patrizio arrived the next morning to take her home Keira could tell something was wrong. He kissed her perfunctorily and, other than guiding her out to the car with his hand on her elbow, refrained from touching or speaking to her as he pulled out of the hospital car park to begin the journey home.

'Is something wrong?' she asked when she could stand the silence no longer.

His hands were white-knuckled around the steering wheel. 'I take it you did not see this morning's paper,' he said through tight lips.

Keira felt a flutter of unease brush over the floor of her stomach. 'No…I was in the shower when the volunteers' trolley came around.'

He drew in a breath and, reaching behind him, took the newspaper off the back seat and handed it to her. 'Did you tell anyone of your earlier suspicions over the paternity of the baby?' he asked.

She looked down at the incriminating headlines and cringed in despair. 'Oh, no…'

'Is that a yes or a no?' he asked in a clipped tone. 'Or perhaps it's an I don't remember.'

She flinched as if he'd struck her, the colour draining from her face.

'Damn it, Keira,' he said through clenched teeth. 'Is this never going to go away?'

She bit her lip until she tasted blood. 'I'm sorry…I'm *so* sorry…'

He let out a rusty sigh and reached for one of her trembling hands and brought it up to his mouth, his lips moving against her skin as he spoke. 'Forget about it, *cara*. It is what we both have to do now—forget about it.'

'Marietta has made you some chicken broth,' Patrizio said once they were inside the house. 'I will have her bring it up to you in bed.'

'Thank you…'

'Until you are feeling better, I will be sleeping in one of the spare rooms,' he said after a tiny pause. 'The doctor told me you need to rest.'

Keira felt her chest tighten painfully but didn't say anything in response. She made a movement of her lips that could have passed for a grateful smile and moved towards the stairs.

'Wait, Keira.' He came over to her and lifted her gently into his arms, carrying her effortlessly up to the master bedroom where he laid her on the bed.

He straightened from the bed, his expression completely devoid of emotion. 'Rest for now. I have to pick something up from my office but I should be back in an hour or so.'

She watched him leave the room, her heart aching for what she wanted but couldn't have.

His trust.

An hour after he had left Marietta came in with a worried look on her face. 'Keira, you have a visitor but I am not sure Signor Trelini would like you to see him,' she said. 'He gave me strict instructions on who was and wasn't allowed to see you.'

'Who is it?'

'Garth Merrick.'

Keira sat upright and brushed back her hair. 'It's all right, Marietta,' she said. 'I would like to see him.'

'Signor Trelini told me never to let that—'

'Signor Trelini is not here at the moment and if I want to see a friend of mine there is nothing he can do to stop it,' Keira said with determination. 'Besides, I have something important to say to him.'

Marietta blew out a sigh and went out, returning a short time later with Garth a few steps behind. 'I will wait outside in case you need me,' she said with a pointed look.

'Thank you, Marietta,' Keira said, 'but I would like to have some privacy, if you don't mind.'

The housekeeper gave Garth a chilly up and down glance and stalked out.

'Sorry about that,' Keira said. 'She's not normally like that.'

'It's all right…' Garth said, looking uncomfortable. He took in a deep breath and began, 'I had to see you before I left, Keira.'

'It's not yours, Garth,' she said without preamble. 'I was already pregnant before that night. Two weeks pregnant, to be exact.'

'I know,' he said, raking an unsteady hand through his light brown hair. 'That's why I'm here.'

Keira remained silent.

His throat looked as if he was trying to swallow something far too big for his oesophagus. 'I have something to tell you that is going to totally shock you,' he said.

Still she stayed silent but she could feel her heart skipping a beat every now and again.

'Keira…I want to tell you about my fiancée.'

'I'm happy for you, Garth,' she said with an attempt at a genuine smile. 'Really. It's great news. And moving to Canada will be wonderful for you. You've always wanted to travel.'

He gave her a twisted look. 'You still don't understand, do you?'

She looked at him blankly. 'Understand what?'

He let out a long breath. 'Keira, for most of my teenage years I struggled with lots of issues. My father being a high profile politician like yours gave us a lot in common, but it was more than that. You were always there for me. There was hardly a thing I couldn't discuss with you. I've never had a friend closer than you.'

'Thanks...I felt like that too.'

Garth looked down at his hands for a moment. 'I know...but there was one thing I didn't discuss with you; in fact, I couldn't discuss it with anyone.'

Keira unconsciously held her breath.

He raised his eyes back to hers. 'You don't know how many times I wanted to talk to you about...about how I felt. I've agonised over it for years, trying to pretend it wasn't how I was, but I can't live like that any more.'

She frowned as she tried to follow him. For a moment she even wondered if he was going to confess to having been in love with her all these years. 'Are you saying what I think you're saying?' she asked, her heart beginning to chug in dread.

His throat moved up and down convulsively. 'Keira, I am in love with someone, deeply in love with them, the way I wanted to be in love with you but could never be.'

Relief deflated Keira's chest. 'That's great...that's really great. I told you, Garth, I'm thrilled for you. Really thrilled.'

'He's a man.'

Keira's eyes widened. 'You're...*you're gay?*'

He nodded. 'I've been struggling with it since I was fourteen or so. I haven't told my parents yet. Can you imagine what they'd say? I'm their only child, the only son to carry on the Merrick name. Since I was born they've had it all planned out. I'm expected to settle down and get married, and yet I am never going to give them the grandchildren they so desperately want. That's why I'm moving to Canada. I just can't bear to tell them face to face.'

'But what has this got to do with me?' Keira asked. 'I mean I'm fine about you being gay, really. It's not as if it's a choice, right?'

He shook his head. 'I wish it was…I really do. It would have been so much easier all round if I had fallen in love with some nice girl like my parents wanted. I tried many times. I've slept with several women but it just didn't feel right.'

'Garth…' She moistened her desert-dry lips. 'About that night…the night we slept together…'

His eyes met hers, the pain in them unmistakable. 'We didn't sleep together, Keira.'

She blinked at him, her heart coming to a standstill. 'You mean we didn't have…have sex?'

A dull flush flooded his cheeks. 'You had been sick all over your clothes so I helped you have a shower and put you to bed while I washed your things. I had nowhere else to sleep so kept to my side of the bed.'

'But you said we—'

'I know what I said. When Patrizio arrived I was angry at him for hurting you by having an affair. Of course I didn't realise until a couple of days later that he hadn't been involved with that woman but by then it was too late.'

'But…but why didn't you say something?' she asked. 'Why let me believe for all this time that I had a one-night stand with you?'

'I thought I was doing you a favour,' he said. 'You were so upset when you came around that night. You said you hated Patrizio and wanted a divorce. Later on when I'd thought about it a bit more I came to realise it was probably just a heat of the moment thing on your part, but when the newspapers got wind of it I couldn't retract what I said had happened.'

'But why not?' she asked, her expression contorted with anguish.

He gave her an agonised look. 'Keira, my father had promised me a generous financial hand with setting up my furniture design business; it was a chance to take my designs overseas. I knew that if he found out I was gay he would withdraw his offer. The press did me a favour by naming me as the man who was your lover.'

'But what about what it did to me?' Her voice came out as a tiny croak of despair.

He swallowed again. 'I didn't realise until a few days later what it had done to you. Like you, I was convinced Patrizio was having an affair. I thought I was helping you by teaching him a lesson.'

Keira was still trying to take it all in. 'But that night…the bed was…I was sure we'd…you know…been intimate….'

'I wanted you to believe that; I thought I was helping you as well as me.'

She looked at him, her mind reeling, the blood roaring in her ears. 'I didn't do it…'she said, her voice sounding as if it were coming from a long way off. 'I wasn't unfaithful to Patrizio…All this time I've hated myself for something I didn't even do…'

'Please forgive me,' Garth said. 'I have been such a coward about this. But all that is going to change now. I talked to my partner, Mark, about it. Once we've had our commitment ceremony in Canada we're going to tell my parents about our relationship. Mark also helped me to see I had to fix things for you. That's how I came up with the idea of contacting Jamie and Bruno.'

Her eyes came out on stalks. 'It was *you?*'

'Yes. I heard you had been unwell for weeks and I suspected that deep down you were unhappy about splitting up with Patrizio. I wasn't sure if it would work but I had to give it a try. The boys were great about it. Bruno was convinced it would work. He said Patrizio hadn't got over you. He was sure he still loved you but wouldn't admit it.'

'But aren't you forgetting something?' Keira asked. 'Patrizio won't take my word for it. I don't even remember that night.'

'That was probably because of the narcotic painkillers I gave you,' he said. 'I didn't realise you shouldn't have them with alcohol but by then it was too late. Mixed with even the smallest amount of alcohol they have an amnesiac effect. You didn't drink much but it must have been enough to knock you out for the count. You went to sleep and I couldn't wake you for hours.'

'And Patrizio saw me in your bed.'

He flushed again. 'I know. I should have told him the truth but I wanted him to believe you had slept with me. I wanted everyone to think I had slept with you to take the heat off my relationship with Mark. I was so confused. It's taken me years to accept my sexuality. I'm sorry, Keira. I hate to admit this, but even if I had known you weren't really serious about breaking up with Patrizio I probably wouldn't have come clean until now. I had too much at stake. It was only when you told me you were pregnant and you thought it could be mine that I realised I would have to eventually tell you the truth. This morning's paper made me realise how hard this has been, not just for you but for Patrizio as well. That's why I am here now.'

Keira felt her whole body begin to tremble. 'How could you do that to me, Garth? How could you stand by and watch my whole life fall apart over the last few months and not do something to clear my name?'

'I know it must seem horribly mercenary to you, but I did what I felt was the right thing at the time,' he said. 'I realise now it was wrong and I've tried to undo the damage. I just hope it's not too late.'

Tears fell unheeded from her eyes. 'It is too late, Garth. It's far too late.'

'No, it is not,' Patrizio said, pushing the bedroom door open.

Keira could barely see him for the blur of tears but she saw the way Garth stepped to one side, as if afraid that Patrizio was going to tear him limb from limb.

'Please leave—' Patrizio addressed Garth curtly '—Marietta will see you out.'

'I'm sorry,' Garth said, his throat moving up and down in genuine distress. 'I am truly sorry. Like Keira, I thought you were having an affair. I thought I was helping her.'

Patrizio's jaw was tight. 'Right at this minute I am not interested in hearing your apology; I am more interested in delivering my own to my wife. Please leave before I change my mind about rearranging your features for you. I am not a man prone to violence but I can safely say I have never in my entire life been angrier than at this moment.'

'Come this way, Mr Merrick,' Marietta said and ushered Garth from the room and discreetly closed the door as they left.

Patrizio came over and sat on the edge of the bed and, using the edge of the sheet, began to gently wipe the tears from

Keira's eyes. His touch was so very tender that she began to cry all over again, her thin shoulders shaking, tiny hiccupping noises coming from deep inside her.

'Shh, *cara*,' he soothed her softly, stroking the back of her head as he pressed her face to his chest. 'Please do not cry any more. It breaks my heart to see you crying.'

'I—I can't help it…' she said, looking up at him. 'Oh, Patrizio, what have we done to each other?'

Moisture was bright in his dark eyes as they held hers. 'We very nearly lost each other, *tesoro mio*. We allowed other people to destroy what we had. I cannot believe I accused you so vehemently about not trusting me when I did the very same thing to you. I should have questioned Merrick more closely since you didn't remember what happened that night. It would not have taken much to get him to confess, I am sure of it. Instead I walked away and left you to deal with the vicious attacks from the press when all the time you were innocent. I cannot forgive Merrick for that but, even more, I cannot forgive myself.'

'We have to forgive each other,' Keira said. 'I mean…that is if you want to try again…'

He brought her chin up, his dark eyes pinning hers. 'What is this? You think I do not want to stay married to you?'

'I thought you only wanted to take me back because of the baby…You seemed to be struggling with your decision, you seemed distant…and this morning…'

He let out a sigh as he began to stroke her cheek with the pad of his thumb. 'When you were unconscious in the hospital you called out for Merrick. It was like a knife in my gut. I couldn't help feeling you would rather be with him than with me.'

'Oh, God, I can't believe how close we were to throwing it all away again,' she said, burying her head into his chest. 'I was so sad, so lonely at the thought of you leaving me all over again.'

'I have never stopped loving you, *cara*,' he said into the fragrant cloud of her wild hair. 'I realised it almost as soon as you walked into my office that evening to discuss the boys' feud. I felt such a rush of feeling for you that I mistook at first for hate but later realised it was the opposite. But I was too proud to let you see what you did to me. I was content to allow you to think it was simply a physical thing but instead it is much more and always will be.'

He eased her away so he could look into her eyes. 'I am so deeply ashamed of the things I said to you. How you can possibly still love me I will never know. If you were to cast me from your life right here and now it would be no more than I deserve for not trusting you. I can never forgive myself for that. It will be years before I can even think of it without pain, I am sure of it.'

'I feel such a fool for not realising about Garth,' she said as he reached for her again. 'We were so close for so long and yet I never once guessed what he was going through. If only I had known…'

Patrizio's brows moved together in a frown. 'You are ready to forgive him for what he has done to us? How can you even think of doing such a thing? He came close to ruining both of our lives.'

'Yes, but he did what he could to fix it,' she said. 'If he hadn't approached the boys we would be well on our way to being divorced by now. You would never have seen me again and I would have been miserable and alone for the rest of my life.'

He brushed at his eyes with the back of his hand. 'Do not even mention such things, *cara*,' he groaned. 'I cannot bear the thought of how close we were to losing each other. I am never letting you out of my sight ever again. Do you hear me? No more business trips unless you come with me. And as soon as you are well enough we are going to have that second honeymoon. I am going to treat you like a princess for the rest of our lives.'

'Oh, Patrizio, I can barely believe this is real,' she said, smiling up at him. 'Even my parents have been marvellous. They want us to go around for a barbecue when I'm feeling better. A barbecue instead of one of their interminably boring formal dinner parties! Can you believe that? My dad even told me he loved me.'

He smiled and tucked a springy curl behind her ear. 'I am glad he has finally realised what a treasure he has in his beautiful daughter,' he said. 'I hope that one day very soon we will have a little girl with wild curly black hair and violet-blue eyes, a feisty temper, a little pout of a mouth and a delightfully stubborn chin.'

A smile began to spread like bright sunshine over her face. 'So you think we're having a little girl, do you?' she asked.

He pressed a soft kiss to her mouth. 'I am sure of it, *tesoro mio*,' he said and took a coin out of his pocket and began flipping it. 'Which do you want? Heads or tails?'

Keira caught the coin mid-air and smiled back at him as she clutched it tightly in her palm. 'There's no winner or loser this time around. We both have what we want—each other.'

'You are right,' he said, kissing her again. 'But a little girl will be a nice little bonus, yes?'

And, just under five months later, the safe arrival of tiny Alessandra Patrice Marietta Trelini proved him absolutely right.

0108/06/MB131

Coming in January 2008

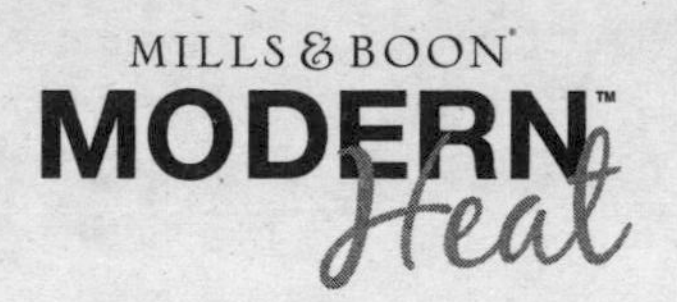

If you like Mills & Boon® Modern™ you'll love Modern Heat!

Strong, sexy alpha heroes, sizzling storylines and exotic locations from around the world – what more could you want?

2 new books available every month

Starting 4th January 2008

Available at WHSmith, Tesco, ASDA, and all good bookshops

www.millsandboon.co.uk

0208/06

SOLD TO THE HIGHEST BIDDER

by Kate Hardy

Jack Goddard is a man who knows what he wants – and he *always* gets it. Right now, Alicia Beresford's not at all happy with his bid for her beloved family home. But Jack is determined to go ahead with his property plans…*and* with taking the alluring Alicia to bed as part of the bargain!

TAKEN BY THE BAD BOY

by Kelly Hunter

Serena Comino was looking for a distraction. Working on a remote Greek island was fun, but nothing changed from one day to the next. Until pilot Pete Bennett flew in… Pete had Bad Boy written all over him! From his carefree attitude and lazy grin to that seductive glint in his eyes, Serena knew she could be in trouble if she fell for this irresistible rogue…